RYLEIGH'S RESCUE

Joyce Byers Hill

Yakima, WA

Books by Joyce Byers Hill

A PLACE CALLED HOPE series:

Diamond in the Rough

JC's Hope

Building Dreams

Ryleigh's Rescue

Dedication

I want to dedicate this book to my dog Uffda, who religiously herds me to the den every morning to write. Even if I don't think I have any words of value. I also dedicate this book to my brother, who insisted the next book had to have a puppy in it.

To my daughter Chereé, my biggest cheerleader, editor, and cover designer. You said I already had all the stories in me; I just needed to sit down at the computer and let them out. I hope you're not tired of designing covers yet.

And to my readers, thank you for returning to *A Place Called Hope*. If you can relate to the characters and have been inspired by their stories, invite your friends to visit *A Place Called Hope*. You know you want to!

Chapter One

Ryleigh Harmon couldn't stop smiling as she drove down the road with her car radio blaring country music. She was heading home. Finally. It felt like she had been away from home for a lifetime while attending college, and then pursuing her master's degree in graphic design. So much had happened during that time. So many family events she was forced to take part in over the phone, rather than in person. So many changes she had missed. But not anymore. She was moving back to Hope, the small town where she was raised. And, God willing, the town where she would someday raise a family of her own.

While growing up in Hope, her dad Travis was the pastor at Hope Community Church. Her mom Meghan and her uncle, Todd Byers, owned and operated Byers Construction, the family business they took over after Ryleigh's grandpa passed away many years before her birth. Now, after being away at school for so long, everything had changed. Both her parents were retired. Her older sister Kaci, and their cousin Aiden, were now the third generation running the construction company. Her brother Josh, known to most people as JC, owns JC's Hope, a youth center for troubled teens, which he runs with his wife Amy.

One of the biggest adjustments Ryleigh would face would be finding where she fits into her much larger family now. Kaci and Jason's twins were ten years old already. Ryleigh felt as if she had missed most of Aaron and Sophie's childhood. JC and Amy's little boy Levi would soon be celebrating his first birthday. Aiden was now married to Bailey, a lady he had met while they both served in the Army. With all the changes in the family, it was hard to believe her cousin's wedding was only a couple of weeks ago. They were married in a double wedding ceremony with Bailey's younger sister Emma and Amy's brother Matt.

Ryleigh hoped to be able to spend time getting to know Bailey and Emma better since they were already firmly entrenched in the family. The sisters had moved over from Seattle after Bailey was hired as the Associate Pastor at Hope Community Church. When Travis retired, Bailey stepped into the Senior Pastor role. JC hired Emma as the business manager at the center so Kaci could concentrate on the family construction business. Bailey and Emma had twin brothers, Wyatt and Spencer, who lived in Seattle but spent a fair amount of time visiting their sisters in Hope. They were already considered part of the family.

All these changes occupied a large part of Ryleigh's thoughts as she drove down the road. But knowing she would soon be home for good kept the smile on her face.

* * *

Lost in her thoughts, and traveling a road she had been driving for several years, Ryleigh, unfortunately, found herself running on autopilot. Luckily, she caught a glimpse of movement at the edge of the road in time to slow down and pull over. She sat in her car, waiting to see if the black object was simply a piece of discarded trash the wind had caught. Then it moved again. Ryleigh got out of her car and began approaching the object that was several yards away. As she got closer to what looked like a small black ball, she heard a faint whimper.

She walked up to the little animal slowly so she wouldn't startle it, talking in a soft soothing voice.

"Hey, little one," Ryleigh said as she reached down to pet the animal.

A tiny frightened nose emerged from the ball of jet-black fur. A baby puppy! A little head raised as she continued talking softly, and two deep brown eyes stared up at her.

"Oh, my!" Ryleigh gasped as she carefully picked up the terrified puppy and pulled it close to her chest. "What are you doing way out here in the sagebrush all by yourself? You can't be more than…what? Six weeks old? Eight?"

Sensing safety, a little tail began wagging as Ryleigh carried the puppy back to her car.

"You must be hungry, little girl."

Holding the puppy in one arm, Ryleigh reached into the back seat where she had tossed the remnants of her fast food lunch. After grabbing the sack, she then climbed into the back seat and sat the puppy safely on the jacket sprawled across the seat.

"Let me see what I can find for you," Ryleigh said as she opened the sack. "I'm glad I wasn't hungry enough to polish off my lunch."

Pulling out a couple of French fries and the remains of a hamburger, Ryleigh broke up a few small bites and put them into her hand. "I'm sure this isn't the best food for you, little one, but it's better than nothing."

After watching the hungry puppy devour the few meager bites of food, Ryleigh reached up to the center console and grabbed her empty drink cup. She tore the cup down, so it was only a couple inches tall, then grabbed her water bottle and poured a small amount of water into the cup.

Holding the water out to the pup, she said, "Now, don't drink it too fast. Just a little bit. You can have more later."

The little ball of fur wagged its tail as it happily lapped up the precious water.

"You know, I can't keep calling you little one," Ryleigh addressed the puppy with a smile. "You were the cutest thing to come out of that field of sagebrush. How about if I call you Sage? Would you like that?"

The puppy looked up at Ryleigh, wagged her tail, and yipped.

"Sage, it is, then," Ryleigh said with a smile.

She picked up the pup and her jacket and got out of the back seat. "Well, Sage, let's get you settled up front for the drive home."

After spreading her jacket out over the front passenger seat, and tucking the puppy safely into the jacket, Ryleigh closed the passenger door, walked around the car, and climbed into the driver's seat. She sat back in the seat with a smile as she started her car. Looking over at the puppy, who had already settled in for a nap, Ryleigh chuckled.

"I hope you like big families, Sage. But don't worry. They're great, and they're all going to fall in love with you. Boy, Dad and Mom are sure going to be surprised when you show up." Then, as an afterthought, Ryleigh added with a laugh, "No, probably not."

* * *

Ryleigh pulled her car to a stop just before turning into the driveway of her family home. She sat, simply staring up at the house, happy to finally be home. She was glad she had decided to move most of her belongings home a couple of weeks ago when she was in town for the wedding. All she had needed to do was tie up a few loose ends, clean her apartment, and gather the last of her things. It would be nice to sleep in her own bed again.

Seeing her parents walk out onto the front deck, Ryleigh put her car in gear and started up the driveway. Her parents were soon joined by Kaci and Jason's twins who spent a lot of time during the summer hanging out with Papa and Grandma. Ryleigh had barely climbed out of her car before the twins ran into her arms.

Sophie wrapped her in a big hug. "Hi, Aunt Ryleigh! I'm so glad you're home for keeps! We missed you!"

"I missed you too, Sophie! A kid in each arm, that's what I've been missing," Ryleigh added as she squeezed Aaron.

"Aaron, you look like you've grown two inches since I saw you at the wedding!"

Aaron smiled and puffed out his chest a bit. "Yeah, I'm trying to catch up to Uncle Matt. Mama said if I keep growing I'll have to get a job to help her buy my clothes!" Then Aaron leaned over and whispered, "I think she was just kidding."

Ryleigh chuckled as she released the kids from her embrace.

Meghan had been patiently waiting to hug her youngest daughter. "I'm glad you had a safe trip, honey. It's going to be nice being able to see you every day."

"It's good to be home, Mom," Ryleigh said with a smile.

As soon as his wife released Ryleigh from her long hug, Travis reached out and pulled his daughter into his arms.

"Welcome home, kiddo," Travis said as he kissed his daughter on the top of her head. "I assume you had an uneventful drive?"

"Well, uh," Ryleigh hedged, smiling. "Maybe not totally uneventful."

Travis stepped back, looked at his daughter, and grinned. "What did you do now, Ryleigh? I recognize that look."

"Well, I did have to pull off to the side of the road once," Ryleigh said as if that explained everything. "I brought someone home with me."

Travis glanced over at her car. "I don't see anyone. Whoever it is must be mighty small."

Ryleigh walked around to the front passenger door and reached for the door handle just as Meghan peeked in the window.

Meghan laughed and said to her husband, "You're not going to believe this, honey."

Ryleigh opened the door, reached in, and pulled out a squirming ball of fur.

Sophie and Aaron were at her side immediately. "A puppy!" they squealed in unison.

Everyone crowded around to pet the happy puppy, who seemed to relish all the sudden attention. The puppy began yipping and wagging its tail happily, then started licking Sophie's fingers.

Sophie laughed and said, "That tickles!"

"Why don't we all go around to the back deck," Travis suggested, "and you can tell us the story. We can unload your car later."

After being cooped up in the car, Ryleigh decided to set Sage down on the cool grass so she could stretch her legs. Sophie and Aaron quickly sat down beside the puppy and began playing with her.

Ryleigh followed her parents onto the deck, sank into one of the deck chairs, and let out a contented sigh. Travis joined his wife on one of the loveseats and simply smiled at his daughter.

"So," Travis began, grinning. "How did you manage to pick up your little hitchhiker? I thought the days of you bringing home strays were over."

Ryleigh laughed as she replied, "Yeah, so did I! But, I guess not."

Turning serious, she continued. "Someone apparently abandoned her alongside the road, out in the middle of nowhere. It was bad enough that she was in a big field of sagebrush. But if she had wandered into one of the wheatfields, she never would have found her way out. She was curled up in a ball at the edge of the road. She was terrified, Dad. Poor baby. When I picked her up, she was so scared she was shaking. Who knows how long she had been out there, all alone?"

Looking out into the back yard, Ryleigh smiled as she watched the puppy chasing Aaron and Sophie around in a circle.

"Luckily I had a little bit of my lunch left in the car," Ryleigh continued. "I broke off some small bites of French fries and a little hamburger and fed that to her. You could tell she was starving. She just gobbled it up. Then I gave her a little water to drink. Once I tucked her into my jacket in the front seat, she curled up and fell right to sleep. She slept most of the rest of the way here."

"You always did have a soft heart for animals, Ryleigh," Travis said. "Especially strays. You just don't have it in you to walk away from an animal in need."

"I know," Ryleigh said with a sigh. "Sorry. I'm sure suddenly having a puppy underfoot wasn't in your plans."

"Ryleigh," Meghan said, "having a soft heart is not a bad thing. Besides, I think the kids will love her."

Aaron and Sophie ran up to the deck, with the puppy nipping at their heels. Sophie stopped, picked up the wiggling puppy, and carried her up onto the deck where they all settled in at Ryleigh's feet.

"What's the puppy's name, Aunt Ryleigh?" Sophie asked as she petted the ball of fur lying next to her on the deck.

"I named her Sage," Ryleigh replied.

"You mean like the sagebrush?" Sophie asked.

Ryleigh smiled. "Exactly like the sagebrush. I found her at the edge of a field of sagebrush."

"Hi, Sage," Sophie said as she petted the top of the puppy's head. The puppy wagged its tail and licked Sophie's fingers again. "I think it's the perfect name for her. Do you like your name, Sage?"

The puppy yipped, much to the little girl's delight.

"She likes it, Aunt Ryleigh," Sophie said, giggling.

"How old is Sage, Aunt Ryleigh?" Aaron asked.

"I don't really know, Aaron," Ryleigh replied honestly. "But it looks like she's probably six or eight weeks old."

"I wonder what kind of puppy she is," Aaron wondered aloud.

"I don't know that either, buddy," Ryleigh said. "I think she may be a terrier-poodle mix. When I take her to the vet to get checked out, I'll see if he knows."

The puppy had crawled into Sophie's lap and was happily licking her fingers again, then settled in for another nap.

Travis smiled over at his daughter as he put his arm around his wife's shoulder. "Well, honey, our daughter has definitely returned home. In true Ryleigh fashion."

Chapter Two

Ryleigh pulled her car to a stop in front of Draper Family Veterinary Clinic at the edge of town. She had known the Drapers her entire life and was a frequent visitor throughout her childhood. She had a reputation for showing up with strays, many of whom the Drapers nursed back to health and rehomed. Some of the strays became permanent family members at the Harmon house. Like Byers Construction, the Draper Clinic was now in its third generation, with the founder retired and his son and grandson running the clinic.

Walking around to the front passenger door, Ryleigh reached in and picked up Sage, holding her close to her chest.

"Let's go get you checked out, Sage. You don't have to be afraid. I'm going to be right with you, and you will love the Drapers."

Kevin Draper, the founder's grandson, happened to be in the front office when Ryleigh walked in. He and Ryleigh were old friends, having gone to school together.

"Hi, Kevin," Ryleigh greeted with a smile.

"Ryleigh Harmon," Kevin said, returning her smile. "I heard you were finally back in town. It's great to see you." Glancing down at the squirming puppy in her arms, Kevin added with a chuckle, "I see it didn't take you long to find another stray. Dad and I were beginning to miss you and all the critters you used to bring into the clinic."

About that time, Larry Draper emerged from an exam room with an elderly lady and her Yorkie. After giving the woman a few last-minute instructions, he patted the top of the old dog's head and wished them a good day.

"Hi, Ryleigh," the middle-aged man said in greeting. "It's been a long time!"

"Hi, Dr. Draper. It's good to see you again."

Walking over to pet the puppy in Ryleigh's arms, Larry Draper asked, "Who's this little one?"

"Her name is Sage," Ryleigh replied.

"Let me guess," the elder Draper began with a chuckle, "you're back in the business of bringing home strays?"

"That appears to be the case," Ryleigh laughed. "Dad and Mom didn't seem to be too surprised. I found her abandoned alongside the road when I was coming home yesterday. I wanted to get her in right away to be checked out."

"That's a good idea, Ryleigh. I'm going to turn you over to Kevin here and he can give her a thorough checkup. I'm about to head out to pick up Dad and take him fishing this afternoon."

"How is Grandpa Max?" Ryleigh asked.

"He's still doing great. He turned seventy-five last month and announced that we needed to go fishing more often. So, since today turned out to be such a beautiful day, I decided to play hooky for the afternoon and take him up to Paradise Lake. I hear the trout are really biting."

"Well, have fun. And tell Grandpa Max I said hi."

"Will do, Ryleigh. And you tell your Dad and Mom I said hello."

Kevin reached over, gently plucked Sage from Ryleigh's arms, and immediately began talking to her in a soft, friendly voice. "Let's go back to the exam room, Sage, and check you over."

As Sage began looking over at Ryleigh with little concerned eyes, Kevin said, "Don't worry, Ryleigh is coming too. She will be right beside you the entire time. But I think you and I are going to become great friends."

Once in the exam room, Kevin got right to work. Before long, he turned to Ryleigh and said, "She appears to be in good health, Ryleigh. Let's go ahead and give her the first set of shots. If she was abandoned, I'm sure she hasn't had any of her shots or anything."

"Thanks, Kevin. I appreciate you being able to get her right in. Do you have an idea how old she is, and maybe what breed she might be? It would be nice to have that information, and I know Aaron and Sophie are anxiously waiting to find out."

"So," Kevin began, "can I assume you plan to keep her and make her a part of the family?"

"Absolutely! The kids have already fallen in love with her."

Kevin laughed as he began filling out a vaccination record for Sage. After completing the card, he handed it to Ryleigh.

Ryleigh smiled when she saw the name Sage Harmon at the top of the card.

"My guess is Sage is about eight weeks old. And I would almost bet she's a terrier-poodle mix. I think you can safely tell the kids you have added an eight-week-old Terripoo to the family."

After handing the puppy back to Ryleigh, Kevin added with a chuckle, "She shouldn't get very big, so I'm sure that will make your parents happy."

"Thanks, Kevin. Well, I'll get out of here and let you get back to work. It was nice seeing you again."

"It was great seeing you too, Ryleigh. Now that you're back in town, maybe we can catch a movie one of these days."

"That sounds great. Take care, Kevin."

After settling Sage back into the front seat of her car, Ryleigh said, "Next stop is the pet store. I need to get you a collar, a leash, and a dog bed. Then we'll head home. I'm sure Aaron and Sophie are waiting for you."

* * *

Although she was in no hurry to do so, Ryleigh thought it was time to get moved into her apartment in town. She knew she had been purposely dragging her feet, but she was enjoying being back home and being involved in family activities. But, maybe it was time. She had been home for nearly a month already as she looked for a job. Now that she finally had one lined up, it was time to get settled into her own place. She would be moving into an apartment in a building Mike Slater owned. Mike had been a close family friend ever since he helped JC get the youth center up and running. He had graciously been holding one of the vacant apartments until she was ready to move.

She was glad she would be living in the same building as Emma and Matt, even though she might not see a lot of the newlyweds. Emma had her hands full managing the business end of JC's Hope, and Matt and Aiden were very busy building houses in a local development, while simultaneously trying to build their own homes and working at Byers Construction. Despite their busy schedules, Aiden and Matt had volunteered to help Ryleigh's dad and Uncle Todd get her moved.

Since the apartment was partially furnished, it didn't take long to get all her things moved. Ryleigh was anxious to get settled in before starting her new job on Monday.

"Are you sure you don't want any help unpacking and organizing?" Travis asked.

"No, I've got it, Dad. Thanks anyway. I'm just going to get the basics unpacked to make it livable, then I'll be back over to the house later this afternoon. There's no way I'm going to miss another family spaghetti feed!"

"Okay, kiddo. Just give me a call if you need something."

"I will. Thanks, Dad."

After having spent the past three weeks at Ryleigh's parents' house, where Aaron and Sophie kept her entertained, Sage didn't seem very impressed with the new living arrangements. Ryleigh worried about how the puppy would adapt to apartment life but felt it would all work out okay. Once she started work, she would be dropping Sage off at her mom and dad's house for the day where she would have the freedom to run in the large, fenced back yard.

While Sage explored the apartment, Ryleigh began unpacking; but her mind was already focused on the upcoming family gathering at her parent's house. It was a tradition in the Harmon/Byers family to have periodic spaghetti feeds where the whole family would gather for an evening of good food, games, and movies. She was looking forward to the first spaghetti feed after moving back to Hope. She was finally home now and was more than ready to make up for lost time.

* * *

The noise of family gatherings was music to Ryleigh's soul. After enjoying another feast of spaghetti, salad, and garlic bread, everyone scattered around the living and family rooms and pulled out an assortment of board games. Kaci and her husband Jason challenged JC and Amy to a game of Trivial Pursuit. Aiden, Bailey, Matt, Emma, and Ryleigh quickly decided they wanted in on Trivial Pursuit, so they abandoned their original plans for Monopoly. Sophie and Aaron stayed busy running around in circles with the puppy. Levi, who had just begun walking, filled the room with his giggles because every time he stood up to walk, the puppy jumped up on him and knocked him down.

Since Mike Slater was considered a member of the family, he attended nearly every family gathering. He was hanging out in the living room visiting with several of the other older adults. They had been discussing how well the new housing development in town was progressing, and how impressed he and his business partner were with Aiden and Matt, who had already built two homes in the development after having built their first home next door for JC and Amy.

"How are you liking the construction industry, John?" Jason asked Matt's dad.

John Phoenix had initially been hired as a laborer to help Aiden and Matt build houses. It was a way to ease him back into the workforce after struggling through rehab. After proving himself, he had been promoted to crew chief and had found his niche.

John shook his head in disbelief. "You know, Jason, I still can't quite believe it. I was always one who shied away from manual labor. But I've got to admit when Aiden and Matt offered me a job helping out with the houses, it changed my life. It gave me a purpose, and I'll always be grateful to those boys."

"From what I hear," Jason began, "you've been a great addition to Phoenix Rising Homes. And there's no doubt that Aiden and Matt have made their mark around town."

Mike nodded in agreement. "Hiring those boys as the general contractor for the development was one of the best decisions Roger and I ever made."

Before long, the young adults pushed the board games aside in favor of visiting and catching up on everyone's lives. JC found his way to the piano in the family room and soon filled the house with music as Sophie danced around with Sage in her arms. Ryleigh went over and joined her Uncle Todd and Aunt Nicole on the sofa, and Mike immediately asked her about her new job.

"I don't start until Monday," Ryleigh replied, "but I'm pretty excited about it. It will be nice to get back to work."

"Are you going to work for Carlson Graphics?" Mike asked.

"Yeah," Ryleigh confirmed. "There are only two places in town that do any design work, and neither of them is very big. Luckily, Carlson was looking for a designer, so the timing was perfect."

"I think you'll like working for them," Mike said. "I've known Bob and Pam for a long time and they're great people."

"When I had my interview with Bob, he seemed very nice. It's not a huge firm, so hopefully they'll have enough work to keep me busy."

"What will you be doing for them?" Mike asked.

"Right now, it sounds like most of what they need is someone to do design work for magazine covers and things like that," Ryleigh replied. "I'm hoping to get into more corporate identity and branding eventually. That's really what I enjoy. But I'll see how things go."

JC wandered into the living room after turning the piano over to Emma, and he joined his wife where she sat on the floor.

"Mike, did you know that Ryleigh designed all the graphics on the building at the youth center?" JC asked.

Nodding, Mike said, "I seem to remember that. I hear the kids talking about them. They are very eye-catching. Perfect for a youth center."

About that time, Levi came toddling over to JC, with Sage tagging along beside him.

"Dada!" Levi said as he launched himself into JC's lap.

Sage began licking Levi and tried to join the little boy in JC's lap.

Amy laughed as she reached out to grab the puppy. "Come here, Sage. You can sit in my lap."

Levi reached over and tugged Sage's little ear. "Puppy!"

Ryleigh had been watching the exchange with a smile. "Amy, your son isn't going to like it when I take Sage home in a few minutes."

"I know!" Amy said, laughing. "Between Aaron, Sophie, and Levi, I'm surprised the puppy can keep up with them."

JC stood while still holding Levi in his arms and said, "Puppies have as much energy as kids do. But we should probably get this little boy home before he runs out of gas completely."

Transferring his son to one arm, JC reached out and helped his wife up from the floor. Levi rested his head on his dad's shoulder, fading fast.

"Are you going home, Uncle Josh?" Aaron asked.

"Yeah, buddy," JC said. "We need to get Levi home and get him to bed."

"Are you leaving now too Aunt Ryleigh?" Sophie asked.

Ryleigh reached down and captured the puppy who was once again running circles around Aaron and Sophie. "Afraid so, kiddo. Sage doesn't even realize she's tired. She'll probably fall asleep before we get out of the driveway."

Levi lifted his head from his dad's shoulder and looked over at Sage with sleepy eyes. "Bye, puppy." And his head collapsed back onto JC's shoulder.

JC chuckled and said, "And with that, we'll tell everyone goodnight. Mom, Kaci, as always, thanks for another fabulous spaghetti dinner. You two are amazing!"

As people began saying their goodbyes and heading toward the door, JC hugged his little sister with his free arm. "I'm glad you're finally home for good, Ry. Levi has already gotten attached to Sage."

Ryleigh looked up at her brother out of the corner of her eye. "Yeah, everyone loves the puppy. What about me?" she asked with an unconvincing pout.

JC winked and said, "Since you appear to be a package deal, I guess we'll keep you too." Then he quickly dodged his sister's slap.

Amy shook her head as she took JC by the arm. "Come on, honey, let's go home before you wear out your welcome. Ryleigh, I'll talk to you tomorrow."

As JC and Amy headed out the front door, a very tired little boy whispered, "Bye, puppy."

Chapter Three

Ryleigh sat in a comfortable chair, alone on the back deck of her parent's home, watching the sun come up. Even though she had her own place now, she spent more time here than at her apartment. This was the home she grew up in. She was comfortable here. Her apartment felt cold and stark, even with Sage running around. This home felt like family. Even though she had been away from her family, she somehow felt like she had a certain sense of direction while she was in college. After completing her master's degree, she felt like she had been drifting.

Her new job at Carlson Graphics wasn't enough to keep her busy, and she felt bored most of the time. Everyone in her family seemed to have found their niche in life. She wasn't quite sure where she fit anymore. Having recently hit her twenty-fifth birthday, she felt like she should be married and have an established career by now. Yet here she sat, staring into a beautiful sunrise, feeling completely unsettled. Even Sage seemed to have settled into her new life.

Ryleigh's eyes drifted to the property next door. Her parents, along with her Uncle Todd and Aunt Nicole, had bought the five-acre parcel a couple of years ago, then divided it so each of their kids would have a lot to build a home on. Her brother JC and his wife Amy lived in the house directly next door, the first house built by Aiden and Matt. Shortly after their double wedding, Aiden and Matt finished building their own homes. Matt and Emma lived on the other side of JC and Amy, while Aiden and Bailey lived on the lot behind them. The back corner lot sat empty. That lot belonged to Ryleigh.

Ryleigh heard the sliding glass patio door open behind her. Travis walked up behind his youngest daughter and kissed the top of her head.

"You're up bright and early this morning," Travis remarked as he sat in one of the loveseats on the deck. "I thought you'd be sleeping in after that late-night movie marathon."

Ryleigh smiled before saying, "I don't think those family movie marathons will ever get old to me. We've been doing that my entire life. There are just a lot more people in the family now."

Travis noticed some of the smile left his daughter's face. "It's true, our family has grown a lot in the last few years. But every addition to the family has brought more joy. It's hard to imagine what our family would be like without them."

Ryleigh simply nodded, turning her attention once again to the empty lot next door.

"Are you okay, kiddo?" Travis asked. "You seem a bit quiet these days."

"I'm fine, Dad," Ryleigh replied as she got up and walked over to sit beside her dad on the loveseat. She snuggled in close, allowing him to put his arm around her shoulder. As soon as Ryleigh changed seats, Sage ran over, jumped up onto the loveseat, and curled up in Ryleigh's lap.

With the small puppy nestled between them, the two sat in silence for several minutes before Ryleigh finally spoke. "I don't know what to do with my life, Dad."

Travis removed his arm from his daughter's shoulder and gently sat her up before he turned to face her. "Exactly what part of your life are you talking about?"

"Everything," she replied with a wry smile. "My job, my empty lot next door. You know, my life."

Travis chuckled before replying. "That's a lot to think about on an empty stomach. Why don't we go into the kitchen? I'm sure your mom has breakfast about ready. You can tell us what's on your mind while we devour a plate of flapjacks." Turning to the puppy who perked up at the word 'breakfast,' Travis added, "Well? Come on, Sage. I seem to recall you have a fondness for pancakes and scrambled eggs."

Meghan was just turning from the stove after piling a plate high with pancakes. Travis walked up behind his wife and leaned over to kiss her before taking the plate from her. He set the plate on the table beside a bowl of scrambled eggs, then pulled his wife's chair out for her. Ryleigh brought a pitcher of orange juice from the refrigerator and filled three glasses before sitting down.

After saying a brief prayer of thanks, Travis turned to his wife, "Ryleigh has something on her mind this morning, honey. It appears she's not sure what to do with her life."

"That sounds about right," Meghan said with a smile. "Every one of you kids went through that right after college. You graduate from high school and head off to college. You know what you're doing. You're going after a degree of some kind. Then once you have the degree, you suddenly realize, 'Now what?' What can we do to help you, Ryleigh?"

"I'm not sure, Mom," Ryleigh replied. "I like my job. I really do. But they don't have enough work to keep me busy. I almost feel bad collecting a paycheck for full-time work when I know I'm not putting in a full day most of the time. As much as I hate the thought of it, maybe I need to move to Seattle where there would be more work for me."

Meghan glanced over at her husband who suddenly had a concerned look on his face.

"Life didn't stop just because I was away at school. I know I probably sound like a whiny broken record, but I've really missed everyone. If I leave again, I'll miss watching Levi grow up, just like what happened with Aaron and Sophie.

"Then there's that vacant lot next door," Ryleigh continued. "Aiden and Matt built beautiful homes for JC and Amy, and themselves. And my lot sits empty. I don't want to leave my family again. But I have a master's degree in graphic design. I need to be able to make a living."

Travis smiled across the table at his daughter. "The first question should be, have you prayed about it?"

Ryleigh chuckled softly and said, "Dad, I've been a pastor's kid my entire life. Of course I've prayed about it. I just don't seem to be getting any answers.

"I need something tangible," she continued. "I don't know how to explain it. It seems like everyone else has found their niche. Kaci has Jason and the twins, and she's managing the construction company. JC owns the youth center and has Amy and Levi. Even Aiden and Matt have their lives figured out. They're both working at the construction company and building houses. And they're married! Matt and Emma are younger than I am. I don't even know what I'm having for dinner tonight!"

"You're also the youngest kid in the family, Ryleigh," Meghan said with a smile. "You don't have to figure it all out the minute you graduate. You wouldn't believe the number of people who think they have their lives all planned out, spend years getting a degree, and then end up not even using it."

"The degree isn't my problem, Mom," Ryleigh said. "I love doing graphic design work and I know I will be using my degree. I'm just afraid I won't be able to make a living if I stay here in Hope."

As Ryleigh helped her mom gather the breakfast dishes and put them into the dishwasher, she released an audible sigh.

"Do you know how much I have enjoyed the little mundane day-to-day activities since I've been home? And being able to be here for Levi's first birthday?"

Travis walked over to his daughter and asked, "What do you want to do, Ryleigh? I mean, deep down, if you could do anything you wanted to do, what would that be?"

Ryleigh leaned back against the kitchen counter and thought for a minute. A small smile crossed her face before she replied. "Ideally, if I could do anything I wanted to do, and do it wherever I wanted, I would work for a big design firm doing what I love. But I would be doing it right here at home. In Hope."

"So," Travis began hesitantly, "what's your next step?"

Releasing a heavy sigh, Ryleigh looked at her parents and said, "I think I need to start looking for a job in Seattle. Carlson doesn't have enough work for me here, and I doubt they ever will. Who knows? Maybe I'll get lucky and be able to find a good job in the Seattle area where they'll let me work remotely. But I need to face the possibility that I may be moving to Seattle."

"Well," Meghan began, "first things first. See what kind of job openings you can find in the greater Seattle area, then go from there. Maybe you won't have to move. If you do have to go over to the west side, at least you will know someone your own age, so it won't be like moving to college where you didn't know anyone. You will at least know Wyatt and Spencer. And whatever you decide, Ryleigh, you know your dad and I will support your decision."

* * *

Ryleigh pushed her chair back from the desk and closed the lid to her laptop. Expelling a heavy sigh, she struggled to accept what she knew lay ahead. After a thorough search, she found several good job opportunities in the Seattle area, but none of them offered the option of working from a remote location. She had three video interviews set up for tomorrow. If any of them went well, she would be driving to Seattle for in-person interviews. One of the jobs was her dream job – if only it allowed her to work remotely from Hope.

Just as she walked away from her computer and sat on the sofa, her cell phone rang. Seeing Spencer's name on the caller ID brought a smile to her face. She had first met Spencer Campbell and his twin brother Wyatt when their sister Bailey got engaged to Aiden. They shared an instant connection and had become friends since the wedding. They didn't see each other in person very often because they lived on different sides of the state, but they talked on the phone frequently and spent time together when the boys came to Hope to visit their sisters.

"Hey, Spence," Ryleigh said as she answered the call. "You're not in town, are you?"

"Hi, Ryleigh. No, I'm just taking a break from work. How goes the job search?"

"There are a lot of design jobs in the Seattle area," Ryleigh replied. "Some of them are great opportunities. Unfortunately, none of them offer remote work."

"Seattle's not so bad," Spencer said, smiling into his cell phone. "You knew that would probably be the case. Like I said the other day, there are a couple of vacancies in our apartment building. One is just across the hall from me and Wyatt. And they allow pets here, so Sage won't be a problem."

"Yeah, I'll keep that in mind. I have three video interviews scheduled for tomorrow. Hopefully, I'll be making a trip to Seattle soon for in-person interviews."

"Hey, I have to go, Ryleigh," Spencer said. "Let me know how your interviews go tomorrow. If you come to Seattle, we'll meet up for lunch or something. It would be great to see you again."

"I'll text you after the interviews and let you know. We'll definitely get together if I make a trip over there."

"Oh, and Ryleigh, good luck tomorrow. You're going to knock them dead!"

Ryleigh laughed as she replied, "Thanks, Spence. Talk to you later."

* * *

The next few days passed in a blur as Ryleigh breezed through the video interviews and juggled her work schedule to squeeze in a trip to Seattle. She had two in-person interviews set up and Spence had graciously offered to shuttle her around Seattle. That relieved a lot of her stress since she wasn't familiar with the Seattle area and didn't care for driving in that traffic.

Sage was already snuggled up on Ryleigh's lap, but Ryleigh reached down and pulled her close to her chest. Snuggling the little furry face against her cheek, Ryleigh said, "Well, Sage, it looks like we may be moving to Seattle. I hope you'll like it there. It will be a big change for both of us, but it should be okay. You already like Spence and Wyatt. Maybe they'll be right across the hall from us. You'd like that. So would I. It will take some adjustment for both of us if we end up moving. But it'll be fine, right? Yeah, it'll be just fine."

Sage looked into Ryleigh's sad eyes and reached over to lick one lone tear rolling down Ryleigh's cheek.

Chapter Four

Travis walked into his daughter's empty apartment and found her sitting in the middle of the floor, holding Sage on her lap. He walked over and sat down beside her.

"This move is going to be harder for you than you thought, isn't it?" Travis asked.

"I knew it wasn't going to be easy, Dad," Ryleigh replied. "But now that I look around at my empty apartment, the reality is starting to sink in. I'm glad I was able to get the apartment across the hall from Spence and Wyatt. Maybe it will feel like there's still family around."

Meghan walked into the living room after taking one last look around the apartment to be sure nothing was missed.

"You're always going to have family around, Ryleigh," Meghan said. "Whether you live in Seattle, Hope, or anywhere else, your family will never be far away. And you know you always have a place at home." She then added with a chuckle, "It's not like your dad and I plan to turn your room into a den or anything. I'm sure you and Sage will be coming home nearly every weekend. At least for a while anyway."

Suddenly, Ryleigh jumped up, having nearly forgotten Sage was curled up in her lap. Picking up the startled puppy and tucking her under her arm, Ryleigh said, "Well, let's do this. We're still planning to swing by to pick up Bailey and Emma, right?"

"Yes," Meghan replied with a chuckle. "They didn't want to miss a chance to see their brothers. Something about Wyatt owing them a lunch."

Travis leaned over and picked up Ryleigh's backpack and started toward the door. "Emma already claimed a spot with Sage in your car. Bailey can ride with me and your mom. That should give everyone plenty of room for the drive."

Ryleigh took one last look around the apartment, then closed and locked the door, handing the key to her dad.

"You'll make sure Mike gets the key, won't you, Dad?"

"Yep, I already told him I would have it."

Holding the squirming puppy up to her face and looking her in the eyes, Ryleigh asked, "Well, Sage, are you ready for a new adventure?"

Sage licked Ryleigh's nose and wagged her tail.

"In that case," Ryleigh said with a smile, "Seattle, here we come!"

* * *

Ryleigh had a few days to settle into her apartment before starting her new job at Mariner Graphics & Design. Having Spence and Wyatt right across the hall eased her loneliness. Both of the guys worked for Microsoft but had the luxury of being able to work from home. That was going to make Ryleigh's adjustment a lot easier, especially since they offered to take Sage during the day once Ryleigh began work. The three had eaten dinner together most nights after Ryleigh stopped by to pick up Sage at the end of the day. Occasionally, Wyatt's girlfriend joined them as well.

After tapping on the door to Wyatt and Spencer's apartment, Ryleigh walked in to find Spence rolling on the floor, being "attacked" by little Sage. Ryleigh put her hands on her hips and said in mock seriousness, "Sage, what have I told you about beating up on Spence? You need to be nice to him, remember?"

Sage launched herself off Spence and began running circles around Ryleigh, who bent down and picked up the hyperactive puppy. With Sage safely cradled in her arms, Ryleigh sat down on the couch. Spence dramatically crawled over to the couch and pulled himself up to sit beside Ryleigh.

"Your dog is a bully, Ryleigh," Spence said, laughing. "She tackles me and won't let me up."

"You poor baby," Ryleigh said without sympathy. "That little five-pound puppy is so tough!"

Spence laughed as Sage jumped into his lap and began licking his face. "Are you planning to go home after work tomorrow?"

"Yeah," Ryleigh replied. "It's been a long first week. I was wondering if you guys wanted to ride over to see your sisters."

Wyatt looked up from his laptop on the desk in the corner of the room. "I'm game. Bailey owes me ice cream from The Creamery."

"Sounds good to me," Spence added. "Now that you have almost a full week behind you, how do you think you're going to like the new job?"

Ryleigh's eyes lit up. "I love it! I really do. Doing corporate branding and identity has always been my favorite part of graphic design. It feels good to be doing that again. And I love the team I'm on. I think we're going to work well together."

"That's great, Ryleigh!" Spence said. "After you have a chance to get settled in at your job, maybe you'll stick around

Seattle one weekend and I can show you the sights. Seattle has a lot of fun things to do."

"Sure, I'd like that, Spence." Ryleigh added with a laugh, "Maybe in a couple of weeks, after easing into this city living."

Spencer leaned over and bumped shoulders with Ryleigh. "I'll make a city girl out of you yet. Once you've seen the city from the top of the Space Needle, there will be no going back."

"Give it your best shot, Spence," Ryleigh said with a chuckle, "but I make no promises."

* * *

After nearly a month of making trips home with Sage every weekend, Ryleigh reluctantly agreed to stay in Seattle and allow Spencer to show her the sights. He had offered to ride home with her every weekend so he could visit his sisters, so the two had a lot of travel time to enjoy each other's company. Spence was quickly becoming an important part of her life, and Sage had become very attached to him. Even though the little puppy loved her time with Ryleigh and Spence, it was becoming harder and harder to take her away from the rest of the family at the end of the weekend. Sage had captured the hearts of Ryleigh's niece and nephews, and pulling her away from them was never easy. Maybe not going home this weekend would give Sage more time to settle in.

Spencer knocked on the door to Ryleigh's apartment and smiled when he heard a little bark. As soon as Ryleigh opened the door, Sage ran happy circles around Spencer's feet, begging to be picked up.

Reaching down to pick up the wiggling puppy, Spence scratched behind her ears and said, "You're going to hang out with Wyatt today, okay?"

Sage licked his face in apparent agreement while wagging her little tail furiously. Ryleigh smiled at the now common interaction, grabbed her bag, and locked the apartment door.

Once Sage was curled up in Wyatt's lap on the couch, Spence and Ryleigh set out for their day of sightseeing.

Hoping to get Ryleigh to fall in love with the city that was now her home, Spence purposely concentrated their first sightseeing trip in downtown Seattle. They spent the morning visiting several of the more popular downtown sights. They checked out the aquarium and the Pacific Science Center before deciding they would have lunch in the restaurant at the top of the Space Needle.

Spence reached over and took Ryleigh's hand as they began walking toward the Space Needle.

"Are you having a good time, Ryleigh?"

Ryleigh smiled as she looked over at him and replied, "You know, Spence, I am. I really am. I have to admit that I probably wasn't giving Seattle much of a chance because I didn't want to leave home again. But I really am enjoying myself. Thanks for taking the time to show me around."

Spence squeezed her hand and said, "It's my pleasure."

He suddenly stopped and pointed up, having just reached the base of the Space Needle. "That's where we're going to have lunch. There's a nice restaurant at the top. It spins around."

Ryleigh looked horrified. "What do you mean, it spins around? I can't eat in a spinning restaurant."

Spencer laughed at the common reaction when newcomers were told about the spinning restaurant. "Don't worry, Ryleigh. You won't even notice it. The restaurant rotates very slowly."

As they traveled up the elevator to the top, Spence said, "You're going to love the view from the top. It's incredible!"

As soon as the elevator doors opened, Spence watched Ryleigh's eyes grow wide as she caught a glimpse of the view. Taking her hand once again, he smiled as he led her over to the windows.

"Let's walk around before going to eat." Pointing toward the nearby mountains, he said, "Obviously, that's the Cascades. And that's a view of Mount Rainier you don't see from the east side of the state."

"Wow!" Ryleigh said in amazement. "It looks completely different than the view I'm used to seeing."

"I know. It doesn't even look like the same mountain, does it? And look, that's Elliott Bay. They have a nice harbor cruise around the bay if you'd like to go later."

"That would be fun," Ryleigh replied as they entered the restaurant for lunch. "Is that what we're going to do right after lunch?"

"Originally, I was going to take you to Pike Place Market after lunch. They have lots of cool little shops, and you can watch them toss fish."

Spencer laughed at Ryleigh's raised eyebrows. "But we'll save Pike Place for another day. It can easily be an all-day venture. Since you're an artist, I think you would appreciate the Chihuly Garden and Glass Museum. It's filled with blown glass by local artist Dale Chihuly. It's truly remarkable. When you look at the intricate flowers and things, it's hard to believe it's all made of glass. Then maybe we can end the day with a cruise of the harbor."

"That sounds great. I'll just let you be the guide. After all, this is your city."

After a wonderful lunch, Spencer once again took Ryleigh by the hand and led her through the blown-glass museum. He couldn't stop smiling at how amazed she was at the glass art. He knew her artist's heart would appreciate the incredible talent involved in creating such beautiful pieces.

The weather was perfect for the after-dinner cruise of Elliott Bay. Ryleigh thoroughly enjoyed seeing the Seattle skyline from the water. Seeing the Cascade Range, punctuated by majestic Mount Rainier in the background, made her appreciate Spencer's love of the city. The cruise ended just as the sunset was at the peak of its glory.

As they stepped off the boat, hand in hand, Spence pulled Ryleigh close as they gazed into the sunset. "Did you have a good time today, Ryleigh?"

Ryleigh rested her head on his shoulder as she squeezed his hand. "I did, Spence, thank you. I'm glad you brought me downtown. It gives me a new appreciation for Seattle. It's still not home, but I can certainly see why you like it here."

"For however long you live in Seattle," Spence began, "I want you to enjoy it. Thanks for giving it a chance."

Ryleigh looked into Spence's eyes and could see his complete acceptance. He knew in his heart that keeping her in Seattle would be a tough sell. But he was determined to show her some of why he loved the city and was willing to let the chips fall where they may.

Chapter Five

A few weeks later, Ryleigh and Spencer were returning to Seattle after another weekend back in Hope. Ryleigh glanced over and smiled to see Sage fast asleep in Spencer's lap in the passenger seat.

"Hey, Spence," Ryleigh began, "can I talk to you for a minute?"

Spence looked around the car and grinned. "We seem to be the only people here, so I don't see why not."

Ryleigh hesitated, and Spence could see she was suddenly nervous. He wondered what was on her mind because she had been uncharacteristically quiet on this trip.

He reached over and put his hand on Ryleigh's arm. "I was just kidding, Ryleigh. You should know by now you can always talk to me. What's up?"

"Would you say I've given Seattle a fair chance?" Ryleigh asked.

"You really don't like Seattle, do you?" Spence asked in understanding.

Still, Ryleigh hesitated. "It's not that I don't like it. And I certainly appreciate you making the effort to take me around to see the sights. I think Seattle is a great place to visit."

"But you wouldn't want to live there, right?" Spence finished her thought.

"You must really think I'm flighty, huh?"

"No, Ryleigh, I don't think you're flighty. I think, deep down, you know exactly who you are, and you know what you want. You didn't like being away from your family all the years you were in college. You finally made it back home, then had to move away again. You're unhappy. I understand that. I knew it was a long shot hoping you would fall in love with Seattle. So, to answer your question, yes, I think you gave Seattle a fair chance. What is it they say? You can take the girl out of the country, but you can't take the country out of the girl?

"My sisters hated it the entire time they lived in Seattle. We grew up in a small town. They never adapted to city life after we moved. They couldn't wait to escape. I'm just glad they were able to move to Hope together. I've never seen them happier. Besides, if they hadn't relocated to Hope, I never would have met you."

Ryleigh looked at Spence and smiled, glad he wasn't upset. And thrilled that he actually seemed to understand.

"Ryleigh," Spence began, "you have to be true to yourself, or you'll spend the rest of your life being miserable."

"That sounds like something Dad would say," Ryleigh said with a chuckle.

"He's a wise man," Spence said, smiling. "You should listen to him."

They were both quiet for several minutes before Spence spoke again.

"So, when are you moving back to Hope?"

"I don't know. I need to talk to my boss. I love my job. It's my dream job. I don't want to give it up just because I miss my family. I need to ask Samantha if there's any chance I could work remotely."

"Do you think that might be an option?"

"I don't know. But I know there's at least one other designer who works remotely part of the time. So, maybe there's a chance."

"Have you talked to your parents about it?"

"Not yet. Before I talk to them, I wanted to see if you thought I had honestly given Seattle a chance."

"Talk to them, Ryleigh. You could live in Seattle for a year, seeing all the sights and experiencing all the city has to offer, and you would still be unhappy. Your heart will always be back in Hope." Then Spence added with a laugh, "Just don't be surprised if I continue making weekend trips over the mountains to visit my sisters."

"Sage would love that!" Ryleigh said with a chuckle.

"And what about you?"

"I sure wouldn't complain about it!" Ryleigh said as she flashed the biggest smile Spence had seen from her all weekend.

* * *

After stressing over the situation for two days, Ryleigh finally summoned the courage to schedule a meeting with her boss. She honestly had no idea what to expect, but was glad she had always gotten along with Samantha.

She stood outside Samantha's closed office door for several seconds before finally knocking. When she heard Samantha's reply, she opened the door and walked in.

"Good morning, Ryleigh," Samantha greeted. She pointed to a chair in front of her desk and said, "Have a seat and tell me what's on your mind."

"Good morning, Samantha. I hope I'm not bothering you."

Samantha chuckled and said, "You're actually giving me a wonderful excuse not to attend another boring meeting. So, what's up?"

Ryleigh hesitated before saying, "I've been trying to figure out the best way to say this, but I don't think there *is* a good way. So, I'm just going to say it and we can go from there.

"Sam… I want to move back home. I'm just not happy here. I don't mean here at Mariner Graphics. I mean here in Seattle. I absolutely love my job. But I just can't seem to adapt to city life. And I realize this probably sounds silly coming from someone in my mid-twenties, but I miss my family."

Samantha sat back in her chair and smiled. "I wondered how long it would take you to realize that."

Ryleigh looked at her boss in surprise. "You mean you knew I didn't like living in Seattle?"

"Of course," Samantha replied. "Ryleigh, I'd like to think we've gotten to be pretty good friends over the past few months. You talk about your family all the time. I know they're your lifeline. Besides, there's no shame in not liking city life. I don't like it either. That's why I commute every day. It makes for longer days, but the tradeoff is worth it for me."

Ryleigh sank back in her chair, relieved that her boss understood.

"So, now we discuss how we can move forward," Samantha said. "Ryleigh, I'm going to be honest with you. I don't want to lose you. In the short time you've been a member of my team, you have become one of our best designers. You are incredibly talented and we're lucky to have you. If we can work out a solution that would work for both of us, are you willing to stay?"

"What did you have in mind?"

"Well, one of the biggest advantages of the technology industry is that a lot of jobs can be done from anywhere. You have a good head on your shoulder, and you're very conscientious. You don't need me breathing down your neck every day to make sure you get your work done on time. If we can set you up with everything you need to be able to work from home, your home could be anywhere. You could live here in Seattle, or you could live back in Hope."

"Really?" Ryleigh asked with excitement. "You'd be willing to do that for me, Sam?"

"Absolutely, on one condition. You would need to be willing to come into the office occasionally when needed."

"How often do you think that might be?"

"It's hard to say, but I don't see it being necessary more than probably two or three times a month. Would that work for you?"

"That wouldn't be a problem at all. Thanks, Sam. I was hoping for some kind of work-from-home solution. You won't regret it. I promise."

"I know I won't. Head on back to your workstation, take a breath, and I'll go talk to the guys in IT. I don't see any reason why they can't get everything you need to set up your home office within a few days. You can begin making arrangements to move, I'll take care of things on this end, and you should be up and running from Hope in a couple of weeks."

Ryleigh stood and shook her boss's hand. "Thanks again, Sam. Be sure to let me know if you need any other information from me."

"I will," Samantha said. "Oh, and Ryleigh, one other thing. Never lose sight of who you are. Your heart has always been in Hope, and I want nothing more than for you to be happy."

Ryleigh chuckled before saying, "You're the second person to tell me that in the past few days."

"Well, maybe someone's trying to tell you something," Samantha smiled. "I've never been to Hope. Maybe one of these days I'll take a long weekend and go check it out. I'd love to meet the family who could successfully steal away my best designer."

Leaving Sam's office with a smile on her face and a song in her heart, Ryleigh knew the next order of business would be calling her parents tonight.

* * *

Spence had stopped off for Chinese take-out food to share with Ryleigh so they could have dinner out of the way before she called her parents. He sat down beside Ryleigh on the sofa and Sage immediately jumped into his lap and curled up for an after-dinner nap.

Ryleigh was nervously turning her cell phone over and over in her hand.

Spencer reached over and put his hand on her hand to stop the fidgeting. "Ryleigh, just call them. Your parents are very supportive. They will want you to do whatever it is that makes you happy."

Letting out a heavy sigh, Ryleigh said, "Okay, here goes."

Meghan picked up the call on the first ring.

"Hey, Mom," Ryleigh began. "Is Dad around? I need to talk to both of you."

"He's sitting right here beside me," Meghan replied. "Let me put the call on speaker. Is everything okay, honey?"

"What's up, kiddo?" Travis asked. "Are you okay?"

"Hey, Dad. Yes, I'm fine. Actually, I'm probably better than I've been in several months."

"That's great, honey!" Meghan said. "So, what's on your mind?"

Hesitating only for a moment, Ryleigh asked with a chuckle, "So, have you and Dad turned my room into a den yet?"

"You know we would never do that," Meghan said. "You will always have a place here at home."

"Well, I don't know," Travis said with unconvincing disappointment. "I was hoping to turn it into a workout room."

"Dad! We all know you get plenty of exercise. You, of all people, certainly don't need a workout room."

Travis laughed. "I guess you're right. Okay, your room is still up for grabs. Are you going to come home for a few days?"

"Actually …" Ryleigh said slowly, looking over at Spence for moral support. "I'm going to move back home."

"You are?" Travis asked hopefully.

"I'd like to. If it's okay with you guys."

"Ryleigh," Meghan began, "you know you always have a place here at home. This is your home too, honey. And it will always be your home. We'd be thrilled to have you back in town."

"So," Travis jumped in, "tell us what's going on. How did all this come about?"

"I just don't like living in the city," Ryleigh said honestly. "Don't get me wrong, I love Seattle from a visitor's standpoint. But I'm just not happy living here. It's not who I am. Sam said she doesn't want to lose me. So, she's going to set me up with a home office and let me work remotely."

"That's great, Ryleigh!" Travis said.

"I would still have to go into the office occasionally, as needed. But Sam said that would probably only be two or three times a month, so that's not bad."

"How soon will you be moving?" Travis asked. "Do you need me to come over and give you a hand hauling things back home?"

"I gave notice to the landlord this morning. Since I was renting on a month-by-month basis, it's not a problem. Sam said the IT guys will probably have everything I need in a few days. I don't plan to come home this weekend so I can get things packed up, so I'll probably move home next weekend. Spence seems to think we can get everything into my car and their car, so you won't need to make a trip over here. Wyatt and Spence plan to come over to help with the move and see Bailey and Emma."

After another fifteen minutes on the phone, discussing the details and making plans for setting things up so Ryleigh could share the den with her dad, Meghan asked, "Are you happy, Ryleigh? It sounds like this is turning out to be exactly what you had hoped for. You wanted a good job with a great company. But you wanted to be able to work from home."

"I know, Mom. Isn't it great the way it's working out?"

"This is going to make three little kids very happy," Travis said with a laugh. "Sophie and Aaron told me the other day that they've been praying every night that you and Sage will move back home. Of course, kids being kids, they all miss Sage when you go back to Seattle after the weekend. But this morning, Sophie told me that she really misses Aunt Ryleigh."

"Well, Dad, you can tell all three of the munchkins that Sage and I will be moving home for good in less than two weeks."

"God is good, Ryleigh," Travis said.

"All the time, Dad. All the time."

Chapter Six

It wasn't easy, but Ryleigh had managed to pack all her belongings into her car and Spence's car. She was used to not having all her things in one place. It seemed like her life had been split between two different locations forever. But once she made this move back home, everything she owned would be in Hope. That thought made her smile and she gave her car door a satisfied slam.

Turning to Spencer, she said, "I think that's everything. I'm still amazed we got it all in two cars."

"Oh, ye of little faith," Spence said in mock surprise, clutching his hand to his chest. "Have you forgotten that I am a Tetris expert? Fitting puzzle pieces together is in my DNA. I had no doubt we could make everything fit."

Ryleigh walked over and hugged Spence. "Thanks for the help, Spence. You and Wyatt saved Dad a trip to Seattle."

Spence pulled her into a tight embrace and said, "It's our pleasure. You know, I'm really going to miss seeing you every day."

"I'm going to miss you, too. But we'll talk on the phone, and you know you guys will be coming over to see Bailey and Emma all the time."

"My sisters may be the excuse. But I'll really be going over to see you."

Spencer looked down into Ryleigh's deep brown eyes, and she thought for a moment he was going to kiss her.

"Hey, guys," Wyatt said as he walked up behind them. "Oops, sorry. Didn't mean to interrupt."

Spence released Ryleigh from his embrace and said, "No problem, bro. What did you find out from your boss?"

"He really needs me to finish the last of that project before I leave town," Wyatt explained. "It shouldn't take me more than an hour at the most."

"That's no problem, Wyatt," Ryleigh said. "Sage and I can go ahead and get started over the hill, then you guys can head over once you're finished. I really appreciate your help with the move."

"We won't be far behind you," Wyatt said. "Forty-five minutes or an hour, tops. We should be on the road before you get to the top of the pass."

Spence took Ryleigh by the hand and walked her around to the driver's door of her car. Squeezing her hand, he said, "Drive safe. I'll call you as soon as we hit the road." He then reached across the driver's seat and gave Sage a pat on the head. "You be good, Sage. I'll see you later today."

Ryleigh slid into the driver's seat, Spence closed the door and then stepped back. As she slowly pulled out into the street, he silently wondered how his heart would survive her being on the other side of the state.

* * *

The late spring weather couldn't have been better for a drive over the pass. The skies were clear, and the sun was shining. Perfect weather, in Ryleigh's opinion. As she got closer to the summit, there was more snow along the side of the highway, but the roads were bare and dry. She had been listening to some of her favorite worship music, but had it playing softly so it wouldn't wake Sage. She knew in her heart that God was leading her back home. Back to her family.

She had never been afraid to try new experiences, which was one of the reasons she moved to Seattle. But she had never felt settled about the decision and secretly knew it had been a mistake. She also had to admit that being able to spend more time with Spencer made the move a more attractive option.

Spencer. Their friendship had grown over the past year, and he had become very important to her. Up until their first sightseeing trip in Seattle, she wondered if he thought of her as simply a friend. That day seemed to change their relationship and nudged it into the area of being more than just friends. She thought back to earlier this morning, a little over an hour ago, and was certain he had planned to kiss her. Then Wyatt walked up. The moment may have been lost, but the feeling remained.

The ringing of her cell phone broke into her thoughts. Glancing at the display on the dash, the caller ID showed it was Spence. She pushed the button to answer the call on her Bluetooth.

"Hey, Spence. Are you guys on the road yet?"

"Hey, Ryleigh. We're just getting started now. It took Wyatt a little longer than he thought to finish things. So, we're probably about an hour and a half behind you. How has the drive been?"

"It's been a beautiful drive. The weather is perfect, and the roads are all bare and dry. I'm just coming up on a place to let Sage out for a few minutes. Is Wyatt driving, so you can keep talking?"

"Yeah. Do you need to call me back?"

"No, that's okay. I'm just parking now. Let me switch the phone over and we can keep talking." Ryleigh walked around the car and opened the passenger door to get Sage. In the distance, she heard a mournful howl.

"What's that sound, Ryleigh? Was that Sage?"

Ryleigh chuckled and said, "No, she's still in the car. That's probably a coyote."

"Are you sure it's safe to get out there?"

"Oh, yeah. That coyote is probably a long way from here. Their howls really echo in the hills."

Sage suddenly bolted from the car before Ryleigh had a chance to fasten her leash.

"Sage! Come back here!"

Still holding her cell phone, Ryleigh took off running after Sage, who had already started down the hillside, dodging rocks and scampering over fallen logs.

"Ryleigh! What's happening?" Spence yelled into the phone.

Trying not to lose sight of Sage, Ryleigh lost her footing on the steep slope. She began tumbling down the hill, and her cell phone flew out of her hand. The last thing Spence heard before the phone went dead was Ryleigh yelling, "Sage! Nooo!"

Spencer turned to his brother, who had a look of panic on his face. "What are we going to do, Wyatt? I have no idea where Ryleigh is."

"Try calling her back," Wyatt replied, his knuckles suddenly white from his tight grip on the steering wheel.

Spence tried calling Ryleigh three more times, but none of the calls went through.

"Call Travis, Spence," Wyatt said, trying not to join in his brother's panic.

"Good idea," Spence said, and immediately punched in Travis's number on his cell phone and put it on speaker so Wyatt could hear the conversation.

Travis answered the call on the first ring. "Hey, Spence. How's the drive going?"

"Something happened to Ryleigh!" Spence practically yelled into the phone. "And we don't know where she is!"

"Whoa!" Travis said. "What do you mean something happened to Ryleigh?"

"Wyatt and I are about an hour and a half behind her. We were talking on the phone, and she stopped to let Sage out for a few minutes. It sounded like a coyote was howling, and I think Sage jumped out of the car and took off. Ryleigh must have started running after her. The last thing I heard was Ryleigh yelling, 'Sage, nooo!' Then her phone went dead. I tried calling her back, but the calls didn't go through. What are we going to do, Travis? I don't know where she's at."

"Okay, hold on a minute, Spence," Travis said, as he turned to his wife. "Honey, call Todd. Tell him something has happened to Ryleigh. I need him to come over right away so we can head up the pass."

Taking a deep breath, Travis turned his attention back to his phone. "Okay, Spence, here's what I want you to do. You and Wyatt keep driving up the pass. Keep an eye out for Ryleigh's car. We have location sharing on her phone because of all the driving she does. I should be able to pinpoint her location by her cell phone. As soon as I figure out where she is, I will call you right back. I'm going to bring Todd with me so we'll have plenty of help for whatever may be going on.

"Spence, don't worry. We'll find her. And Wyatt, drive safe. I'll talk to you in a few minutes once I pinpoint her location."

As soon as Travis disconnected the call, he pulled his worried wife into his arms. "She'll be okay, honey."

Travis was searching for Ryleigh's location on her cell phone just as Todd burst in the front door. He immediately pulled his sister into his arms as he looked over Travis's shoulder.

"Okay, I've got it!" Travis said. "She's on this side of the summit, so we'll probably get to her before the boys do. Todd, will you drive so I can call Spence back?"

"You bet!" Todd replied. "Let's go!"

Todd gave his sister another hug. "We'll find her, sis. Don't you worry."

Travis kissed his wife and said, "I'll call you as soon as we find her. Don't worry, honey. Throw a few prayers up. God will protect her."

Meghan gave her husband a weak, watery smile and said, "I've been doing that ever since you got the call. Drive safe, you guys. And call me the minute you know something." As they went to the front door, Meghan stopped at the entryway closet, grabbed a couple of warm blankets, and thrust them into her husband's arms. "You may need these."

After another quick peck on his wife's cheek, Travis and Todd ran out the door to Todd's pickup.

Chapter Seven

Ryleigh tumbled quite a ways down the hillside before she stumbled over some rocks, dislodging them. She came to a sudden stop when her foot got wedged between two large rocks. She tried to get up before she realized her lower leg and foot were trapped. Sitting up, she attempted to push the smaller rock off her foot. It wouldn't budge. She grabbed her leg just below the knee and pulled, hoping to dislodge her foot, but knowing in her heart it was hopelessly pinned between the rocks.

"Sage!" Ryleigh yelled into the wilderness, her voice echoing through the canyon below. "Sage, where are you, girl? Come, Sage!"

Slumping back onto the wet ground, exhausted, Ryleigh nearly whimpered. "Oh, Sage. Where are you, little girl? Sage…"

After several minutes of lying on the wet ground, Ryleigh could feel the cold dampness begin to soak through her flannel shirt. She sat up to take stock of her situation. Giving a cursory look over her battered body, she realized the tumble down the hill hadn't done her any favors. But she was eternally grateful she had decided against wearing shorts for the drive home. At least she was wearing Levis, a t-shirt, and a flannel shirt, all of which had gotten ripped to some degree in the fall.

"Why didn't I wear my hiking boots?" Ryleigh asked out loud. "Probably because I didn't plan to hike down the mountain," she chuckled to herself. "A jacket would have been a good idea. I guess it didn't turn out to be a good time to take off my jacket for the drive."

Ryleigh called out to the wilderness once again. "Sage! Where are you, baby girl? Sage! I need you!"

Feeling something trickling down the side of her face, Ryleigh reached up to wipe the dirt away and her hand came back covered with blood. "Well, that would explain the sudden headache," she lamented. After realizing she had hit her head hard enough in the fall to have drawn blood, she inspected her body a little closer. Her favorite flannel shirt had been ripped beyond repair, and both her arms were scraped and bloody. Without being able to see her trapped foot, she had no idea what kind of damage had been done to that. She prayed nothing was broken.

She also suddenly realized she had no idea how much time had passed. How long had she been trapped? Where was her cell phone? How much had Spence heard before the phone flew out of her hand? Would he be looking for her? Would he think to call her dad?

Suddenly shivering from the combination of the cool mountain air and her damp clothes, Ryleigh did what came naturally to her. She reached out to God.

"Please, God, help someone find me before it gets much colder. I'm so cold."

Another mournful howl sounded in the distance, causing Ryleigh to quickly add to her prayer. "Protect me, God, from whatever wild animals may be roaming the hills. And please protect little Sage. She means the world to me. I couldn't stand it if something bad happened to her."

Attempting once again, Ryleigh summoned all her strength and yelled, "Sage! Sage! Come here, girl!"

Somewhere in the distance, Ryleigh thought she heard a little yip. Then another.

"Sage! Is that you, girl? Come, Sage!"

The little yips seemed to get closer. Ryleigh's heart soared as it became obvious from the high-pitched little barks that it was definitely Sage, and she was working her way up the hill. Before long, there was a lot of barking. But, wait! Ryleigh recognized Sage's high-pitched bark, but there appeared to be another lower-sounding bark as well. Ryleigh turned her head in the direction of the sound and listened closely. No doubt about it, there was definitely another dog with Sage. Then Ryleigh had a concerning thought. What if it wasn't a dog? What if it was a coyote? It was more likely to encounter a coyote roaming the hills, rather than a dog.

No, Ryleigh thought to herself, *that is definitely Sage's happy bark. Besides, a coyote probably would have attacked a little dog.* Ryleigh shuddered at the possibility.

Ryleigh continued calling out to Sage so the little puppy would be able to find her. A few minutes later, she could hear rustling just downhill from where she was trapped. Suddenly, she saw Sage scamper up onto a moss-covered log, and stand staring off into the distance.

"Sage! Come here, girl!"

But Sage didn't budge from her post on the log. Instead, she released a couple of encouraging barks directed off into the distance. Before long, another dog climbed onto the log and stood next to Sage. Sage nudged the dog on its nose in what could only be described as a message saying, 'Come on, you can do it.'

Within minutes, Sage was at Ryleigh's side and was happily licking her face. The other dog slowly walked over and sank onto the damp ground a few feet away, obviously exhausted. The dog appeared to be some sort of collie, possibly a border collie. He was very malnourished, and his hair was severely matted. The poor guy had probably been lost in the mountains for days. Maybe longer.

"Is that why you took off running down the hill, Sage? Did you hear this poor guy out there? You know, little one, you could have been hurt. And what if the howling you heard had been a coyote and not a poor lost dog?"

Sage just wagged her tail happily and walked over to lie down beside her new friend.

Ryleigh patted the ground beside her and said, "Come here, boy. It's okay. I won't hurt you. I just want to check you out a bit. Not that I can be much help. I seem to be trapped here. So, until someone comes along and finds us, we're all out of luck."

In an act of trust, the collie stood up and slowly walked over to Ryleigh. She reached out and petted him on the head and was rewarded with a wag of the tail.

"I bet you haven't eaten in a while. Let me see if the package of beef jerky I had in my shirt pocket survived my quick trip down the mountain."

Relieved to find the unopened package still in her pocket, she ripped the top off and said, "It looks like our lucky day, guys."

She reached into the package and pulled out a small piece of jerky. Sage wasted no time grabbing the tasty jerky, but she surprised Ryleigh by taking the piece over and setting it on the ground in front of the collie. The collie wagged his tail and quickly devoured the welcome piece of meat. Ryleigh handed another piece to Sage, who once again offered it to the starving dog.

"You're really something, Sage, do you know that?"

Sage simply wagged her tail and lay down beside her friend.

Ryleigh sighed as she watched her amazing little rescue puppy who had such a big heart. Suddenly, she thought she heard the slam of a car door.

"Help!" she yelled up the hill, as both dogs began barking. "Someone help me!"

Having located Ryleigh's car with the passenger door left wide open, Travis had no doubt his youngest daughter was in trouble.

"Ryleigh? Where are you?" he shouted back.

"Dad, is that you? I'm partway down the hill, and I'm trapped. Call Sage, and she'll come to you and bring you down."

"Come here, Sage!" Travis yelled. "Come on, girl!"

Sage quickly scampered up the hill like she had been doing it all her life, barking the entire way. Travis and Todd stood at the side of the road until they caught sight of the little dog. Then Todd grabbed a blanket and both men met Sage before she got up to the road.

As the two men carefully picked their way down the steep hill, Sage ran ahead of them, barking happily.

Tears were running down her cheeks at the sight of her dad and uncle. "Boy, am I sure glad to see you guys! And I'm almost as glad to see that blanket! I'm freezing!"

Todd quickly covered Ryleigh with the blanket, while Travis pulled his daughter into a brief hug.

"Wow, kiddo," Travis said, shaking his head. "It looks like you did a number on yourself."

"Yeah, I know. My foot is wedged in between those rocks, and I couldn't budge them at all."

"Okay, we'll get you out of here in no time. Todd, let's see if the two of us can get one of those rocks to move."

As much as they tried, the rocks refused to budge.

"I'll climb back up to the truck and grab the pry bar and the first aid kit," Todd said as he started up the hill. "In the meantime, why don't you give Meghan and Spence a quick call? Do you have any cell service down here? If not, I could call them when I get back to the truck."

Travis glanced at his phone and said, "It looks like I have service. Only a couple bars, but that should get the calls out."

By the time Todd had worked his way back down the hill, Travis had talked to his wife and filled her in on Ryleigh's adventure, assuring her that their daughter would be just fine. He had also made contact with Wyatt and Spencer and found out they were only about ten minutes away.

Sizing up the situation, Todd placed the pry bar into a strategic location between the two boulders. "The last thing we want to do is have this boulder fall back down onto Ryleigh's leg. I'd suggest that we give it one try, and if the two of us can't do it, let's wait for Wyatt and Spence. That way we'd have one man on the pry bar, two pushing and steadying the boulder, and one to pull Ryleigh free. I doubt she has much strength left to pull herself out."

"Good plan, Todd," Travis quickly agreed. "Let's try it."

After one attempt, it was obvious they needed more manpower.

"Okay," Travis said. "The boys will be here any minute. The four of us can do it."

Todd turned to start back up the hill, and said, "I'll go back up and meet the boys." As he started to walk away, he suddenly noticed the second dog lying off to the side. "Hey, where did that dog come from?"

Ryleigh chuckled weakly, realizing her dad had not noticed the second dog either. "That's the reason I'm in this predicament. When I opened the car door to get Sage, she apparently heard this guy howling in the distance and took off looking for him. I think he's been lost out here in the mountains for a while. He's pretty malnourished."

Travis laughed at the irony. "So, Ryleigh, it looks like your rescue dog also rescues dogs. This could get interesting."

Todd laughed as he climbed up the hill. "I see a lot of paw prints in your future, Travis!"

While Todd waited at the road for Wyatt and Spencer, Travis used the first aid kit to clean up some of Ryleigh's cuts and scrapes. The cut on the side of her head appeared to be the worst one, and Travis knew he would be taking his daughter to urgent care as soon as they got back to town.

"Hey, Dad," Ryleigh said, "do you think you could look around and see if you can find my cell phone? It flew out of my hand when I took my unexpected trip down the mountain." She pointed off to the side, behind where the dogs had settled in for a nap. "I think it's over there somewhere. It rang a couple of times, but I was obviously indisposed and couldn't get to it."

Travis smiled at his daughter's optimistic attitude, and said, "Sure, I'll look around while we're waiting for the boys." Then he added with a chuckle, "Now, don't go anywhere."

"Ah," Ryleigh sighed, "it's going to be great to be back home and get a daily dose of your sense of humor."

Travis located her cell phone at about the same time he heard a commotion up on the road. Looking up the hill, he saw Todd and the two boys heading their way.

"You boys be careful," Travis yelled. "That slope is steeper than it looks. We don't need any more casualties."

With the extra hands, it didn't take long to free Ryleigh's foot from the rocks. Spence wasted no time pulling her into a gentle hug as she leaned on him for support.

Travis had his daughter sit down on one of the boulders so he could examine her lower leg and foot.

"I don't think anything is broken," he reported. "But as soon as we get back to town, we're going to hit the urgent care and get you checked out. That cut on your head may need stitches, and we want to make sure nothing is broken."

"Okay, guys," Todd said. "Let's see if we can get Ryleigh back up the hill in one piece. Now remember, the slope is steep, and it's wet. And she's not going to be putting any weight on that foot until we know nothing is broken. So, it's going to be a team effort."

As the group slowly started up the hill, Travis turned and said, "Well, come on, Sage."

Sage looked over at the other dog and didn't move.

Travis chuckled and said, "Bring your friend along. We're not going to leave him out here after everything you went through to get him rescued."

With that, Sage jumped up, wagged her tail, and urged her friend to follow her.

"Hey," Spence said, looking over at the two dogs. "Where did the other dog come from?"

Ryleigh simply laughed as she leaned against her dad. "It's a long story, Spence. But he's coming home with us."

Once everyone made it safely back to their vehicles, Travis and Spence settled Ryleigh in the passenger seat of her car, and Sage immediately jumped into her lap.

"I'm going to drive Ryleigh's car back," Spence announced.

"I'll follow you in our car," Wyatt said.

Todd lifted the other dog into the back seat of his truck and wrapped him in the second blanket. The dog looked in the direction of Ryleigh's car and whimpered.

"Don't worry, Jack," Todd said as he petted the dog's head. "We're all going to the same place. Something tells me you're going to be around for a while."

As Travis climbed into the passenger seat of Todd's truck, he looked over at Todd and asked, "Jack?"

Todd simply smiled and replied, "Sure, why not? Jack means God is gracious. I think that dog was the recipient of a huge measure of God's grace today."

Travis nodded his head and said, "God is good."

"All the time, buddy," Todd replied. "All the time."

Chapter Eight

Meghan was waiting at the urgent care clinic next to the hospital when everyone arrived. She ran over to Ryleigh's car, opened the door, and reached in to give her youngest daughter a big hug.

"Oh, my word, Ryleigh! What did you do?"

Before Ryleigh could reply, Travis walked up behind his wife and said, "Don't worry, honey. I don't think it's as bad as it looks. But that's what it looks like when you fall down a mountain."

Ryleigh looked at her mom with tears in her eyes. "I ruined my favorite flannel shirt, Mom. This is the one you gave me my last Christmas at home before I moved away to school."

Meghan took her daughter's hand in hers and said, "It's just a shirt, Ryleigh. And, from the looks of it, it saved your arms from being any more scraped up than they are."

Ryleigh's Aunt Nicole, a nurse at the hospital next door, suddenly materialized with a wheelchair, followed by her husband Todd. "Let's get you inside, sweet girl."

"Why don't all of you go in with Ryleigh," Wyatt suggested. "I'll hang out here to keep an eye on the dogs."

Ryleigh looked over at Wyatt and said, "Thanks, Wyatt. Hopefully, we won't be very long."

Spencer had stepped up beside Todd and reached for the handle of the wheelchair. "I can take this, Todd."

Todd smiled and stepped back, letting the younger man take control of the wheelchair. "She's all yours, Spence." Then he winked as he fell in behind the others as they walked into the clinic.

* * *

After about an hour in the urgent care clinic, the group emerged with Ryleigh on crutches and her foot in a temporary boot splint. Luckily, she managed to escape any broken bones on her fall down the mountain. Her ankle was badly sprained and had some minor cuts, and the doctor had instructed her to stay off it for two weeks. Travis had been correct in his assessment that the cut on her head required stitches. The remainder of her cuts and abrasions had been cleaned and would be allowed to heal on their own. All in all, she felt pretty lucky. Now all she wanted to do was go home and change out of the dirty and torn clothes and get into something warm and dry. And she sure wouldn't turn down a nice warm mug of hot chocolate.

Most of the family was waiting at Travis and Meghan's house by the time everyone got home from the clinic. After checking in to be sure Ryleigh was going to be okay, everyone jumped in to get both cars unloaded and all of Ryleigh's belongings up to her room. JC's wife Amy, with Ryleigh's suggestion, dug through her suitcase to come up with a warm change of clothes.

Sitting on the edge of the bed as Ryleigh changed, Amy said, "You sure got lucky, Ryleigh. How you could fall halfway down a mountain and not manage to break any bones is beyond me. You and JC both seem to have guardian angels watching over you."

"God is good, Amy," Ryleigh said with a smile. "That's my only explanation."

"You're right about that. I can't believe how much my life has changed in the last few years. I have no doubt God brought Josh into my life."

There was a knock on Ryleigh's partially open bedroom door, and JC said, "I heard my name mentioned. Is everyone decent?"

"Come on in, JC," Ryleigh replied.

"Hey, Ry," JC began, "now that I know you're okay, I have a strange question for you."

"Most of your questions are strange, JC," Ryleigh said with a laugh. "But, shoot."

"I looked out into the back yard where the kids were playing and saw Levi chasing Sage around in circles. That's perfectly normal. Then I saw Aaron and Sophie sitting on the grass in the shade with another dog. A dog I've never seen before. Am I missing something?"

"That's Jack," Ryleigh replied as if that explained absolutely everything.

"Jack?" JC asked in confusion.

"Well, according to Uncle Todd, that's his name."

"And how does Uncle Todd know this dog is named Jack?"

"Because that's what he named him," Ryleigh replied with another chuckle.

JC shook his head and sat down in the chair in the corner of the bedroom. "Spill, Ry. I need the story because I suspect it's going to be a good one."

"It's really quite simple. Sage jumped out of the car to go rescue Jack. Only she didn't know his name was Jack. That was Uncle Todd's idea. Sage only knew he needed to be rescued. That's why I tumbled down the mountain. I was chasing Sage, who was on a mission to rescue Jack. Only I didn't know that at the time either. So, when Dad and Uncle Todd came to rescue us, he decided Jack was the perfect name for the dog who had been lost in the mountains and rescued by Sage. See? As I said, it's really quite simple."

Amy was still sitting on the edge of Ryleigh's bed and was now laughing at both Ryleigh's version of the day's events and her husband's reaction to the story.

"So, let me get this straight," JC began slowly. "You move away to school. You have no dog. You move home from school, and you suddenly have a dog. You move to Seattle, and you have one dog. You move back home, and you suddenly have two dogs. So, every time you come home, you acquire another dog?"

"See," Ryleigh said with a smile, "now that wasn't so hard. Although, technically only Sage is my dog. Jack is Sage's dog."

JC stood up and started toward the door. He looked back at his little sister, who he loved with all his heart. "Welcome home, Ry. I have no doubt life is about to get very interesting around here."

Amy laughed as both young women stood and started to head downstairs. "You just love torturing your brother, don't you?"

"I'm his little sister," Ryleigh laughed. "It's in my job description."

* * *

It was not unusual for someone from Draper's Veterinary Clinic to make a house call to the Harmon home. At some point during all the chaos of Ryleigh moving home, tumbling down the mountain, being rescued, acquiring another dog, and now being on crutches, she had managed to call Kevin Draper to tell him about Jack. Kevin had quickly agreed to stop by the house the following day to check the dog out and say hello to the Harmon family.

Following Sage's lead, Jack had made himself at home in the back yard. Travis had stopped by the pet store and picked up a doghouse so Jack would have a comfortable place to sleep while they came up with a game plan, knowing full well that neither Jack nor the doghouse was likely going anywhere. Sage, who rarely left Jack's side, insisted on spending the night outside with Jack in his cozy new shelter.

With Ryleigh and Spencer standing nearby, and Sage anxiously looking on, Kevin examined Jack and trimmed off the worst of his matted fur. Once the excess hair was removed, Kevin and Spencer gave the skinny dog a good bath. Before long, Jack looked like a new dog, even though his ribs were more noticeable than they should have been.

Travis walked up beside his daughter as they watched a very happy Sage running circles around Jack, who had opted to curl up on the cool grass after his bath.

"What's the verdict, Kevin?" Travis asked.

"Well, there's no doubt he's one very lucky dog," Kevin said. "He's obviously suffering from malnutrition. Who knows how long he was roaming around lost up in the mountains? Honestly, Travis, if you guys hadn't found him when you did, I don't think he would have lasted more than another couple of days."

"Jack owes his rescue to Ryleigh and Sage," Travis said.

"I have to give the credit to Sage," Ryleigh added. "There's no way I would have known Jack was down there. And I certainly wouldn't have found him. She heard him and didn't hesitate to take off looking for him."

"She's pretty nimble on her feet," Spence said as he watched the two dogs in the back yard. "But she never would have made it down the mountain and found him in that ravine if God didn't have a hand in it." Staring out into the back yard, he added with a smile, "From the looks of it, they've become inseparable."

Kevin nodded his head in agreement. "Amen to that! I think he'll bounce back fairly quickly under Ryleigh's care. I'm sure he'll be getting lots of attention too. Just try to take some of your cues from him as far as when he needs to rest and not overdo it. He's pretty weak, and it will take time for him to regain his strength."

"We sure appreciate you coming over on your day off, Kevin," Travis said as he shook the vet's hand.

"Not a problem," Kevin replied with a chuckle. "Dad and I have been missing the days when Ryleigh would stop by with another critter she found." Looking over at Ryleigh, he asked, "So, Ryleigh, what's your plan with Jack?"

"I'm not really sure yet, Kevin," Ryleigh said. "But he's definitely not going anywhere until I get him nursed back to health. He's been through enough. He doesn't need to be shuffled around right now."

"I agree," Kevin said, nodding. "You've always had good instincts when it comes to animals."

As Kevin gathered his gear and put things back into his medical bag, there was a commotion at the side gate. Aaron and Sophie ran into the yard, followed by their mom. Kaci had hung back a bit and was talking to Mike Slater, who arrived right behind them.

"Now you kids don't be bothering poor Jack," Kaci reminded her rambunctious twins. "He needs to rest."

"We won't, Mom," Sophie said. "We're just going to sit with him and Sage."

"Well," Kevin said, "I'm going to get out of here and let you get back to your family." Patting Ryleigh on the shoulder, he added, "Take care of that ankle, Ryleigh. Don't be chasing those dogs around."

Ryleigh laughed. "I won't be chasing any dogs. That's what I have my niece and nephews for! Thanks for stopping by to check out Jack, Kevin. I really appreciate it."

"No problem, Ryleigh. Just let me know if you need anything."

Kevin turned to Mike and said, "Hey, Mike, it's good to see you. It's been a while."

Mike shook Kevin's hand then reached over and took his medical bag as Kevin grabbed the rest of his things. "Let me help you with that, Kevin."

As they started back around the house to the driveway, Mike asked, "How's your dad and grandpa doing, Kevin? I need to stop in and see them one of these days. Maybe tag along on one of their fishing trips."

"They would both love that, Mike! You really should."

As Mike sat the medical bag on the passenger seat of Kevin's truck, he looked toward the back yard and said, "You put any expenses related to Jack on my tab. I'll take care of it."

Kevin simply shook his head and patted Mike on the back. "You got it, Mike. You're quite a guy. This town is lucky to have you."

"It's no big deal, Kevin," Mike said with humility. "I have the means, and I enjoy helping where I can. Now don't forget to tell Max and Larry that I plan to tag along on one of their fishing trips real soon."

After waving to Kevin as he pulled out of the driveway, Mike headed to the back yard. The kids were giving their undivided attention to the two dogs, so Mike joined the adults on the back deck. He pulled up a chair beside Ryleigh, who had her ankle propped up on a table with a pillow. He sat back in the chair, folded his arms across his chest, and let a grin spread across his face.

"So," he began slowly, pinning Ryleigh with what he hoped was a no-nonsense look. "What's this I hear about you falling off a perfectly good mountain?"

Ryleigh grinned back at this wonderful family friend. "Well, Mike, you see, it all started with a dog. He had been lost in the mountains, and Sage found him. And, you know Sage. She just can't pass up a dog in need. She rescued him and insisted we bring him home with us. What could I do? Sage is pretty persuasive." With that, Ryleigh shrugged her shoulders and grinned even wider.

"So, let's see," Mike began as he rubbed his chin, thinking. "What you're telling me is that you're blaming this whole adventure on that cute little puppy out there in the yard? You fall off a perfectly good mountain because that little puppy was on a rescue mission? And you're also telling me that the puppy you rescued just a few months ago is now rescuing dogs on her own?"

Ryleigh simply grinned and shrugged her shoulders as her family enjoyed Mike's playful side.

"Ryleigh, my dear," Mike said, "if you're going to be falling off mountains and rescuing critters on a regular basis, you may as well hang out your shingle, 'Ryleigh's Rescue', and call it a day."

"Hmmm…" Ryleigh began. "Well, I do have that empty lot next door…"

Chapter Nine

Ryleigh's life was beginning to settle into a more normal routine after her mountain rescue adventure. Several days after her unexpected trip to urgent care, Ryleigh's Aunt Nicole made a house call to remove the stitches from the cut on her head and to pronounce that she appeared to be healing nicely. She survived the two weeks on crutches, refusing her mom's offer to set up a temporary sleeping area downstairs so she wouldn't have to navigate the stairs constantly. She insisted that climbing the stairs on crutches was good exercise. While Spence and Wyatt were in town to help with her move, they got her home office set up so she wouldn't miss any projects at work. The kids fell in love with Jack and had no problem sharing their love and attention with both Jack and Sage. All in all, Ryleigh was happier than she had been in a while and was glad to be back home around her family.

Taking a break from a work project, Ryleigh stared out the den window into the back yard. Aaron and Sophie were chasing Sage around the yard while Levi sat on the grass, resting his head on Jack's back while petting him.

Looking over at her dad, who was working at his desk across the room, Ryleigh said, "Jack seems to be doing really well, don't you think, Dad?"

Travis followed his daughter's line of sight into the back yard. Smiling, he said, "He doesn't even look like the same dog you brought home a few weeks ago. Jack is one very lucky dog. You sure have a knack for knowing exactly what an animal needs. That's a gift, Ryleigh."

"I love animals. That makes it easy to sense what they need."

Still gazing into the back yard, Ryleigh asked, "Do you remember that comment Mike made about hanging up my shingle?"

Travis chuckled softly and replied slowly, "Yes…"

"I've been thinking about what he said."

"Of course, you have," Travis laughed. "And before you go any further, let me just say something. Now that you're back home for good, at some point, you're probably going to want to consider building a house on your property next door. You have almost an acre and a quarter. There is absolutely no reason why you couldn't set aside part of your property for a rescue operation."

Travis looked over at his daughter and saw the familiar smile that had been missing a lot as she transitioned into adulthood.

"You know you want to, Ryleigh. You're a natural when it comes to caring for animals. God blessed you with a big heart. I think you were three or four years old when you rescued that baby bird that fell out of the nest. I knew right then there'd be no turning back. Saving animals is part of who you are. Embrace God's gift and go for it."

"Really, Dad?" Ryleigh said with excitement.

"Really, Ryleigh," Travis laughed. "Besides, Sage has already learned how to pay it forward. You rescued her. She rescued Jack. Before long, I have no doubt she'll have Jack rescuing some other poor neglected critter. Use your gifts,

Ryleigh. And you know your mom and I will support you in any way we can."

"What are we supporting now?" Meghan asked with a chuckle as she poked her head in the den door, with her older daughter Kaci standing behind her. "I was just coming to see if anyone was ready for lunch, and I heard that we're supporting something."

"And I just stopped by to pick up my munchkins," Kaci added, chuckling. "But Mom insisted no one could go home until she fed them lunch. Oh, and I have a little gift for Ryleigh."

Ryleigh grinned and asked, "You have a gift for me? But, Kaci, it's not my birthday or anything."

Handing her little sister a package, Kaci smiled. "Let's just say it's a gift for surviving your tumble down the mountain."

Kaci watched as Ryleigh pulled a pillow out of the gift bag, and her eyes instantly filled with tears.

Looking up at her sister, Ryleigh exclaimed, "It's my favorite flannel shirt! But, how?"

Kaci shrugged and said, "I got it from Mom when she wasn't sure what to do with it. After all, you did a pretty good job destroying it. I took it home and threw it in the laundry. Then I cut off some of the salvageable pieces and made it into a pillow for you. I used the rest of the shirt, along with some batting, to stuff the pillow."

Holding the precious pillow tight against her chest, Ryleigh walked over and hugged her sister.

"Thanks, Kaci," Ryleigh whispered, with tears in her eyes. "You don't know what this means to me."

"Yes, Ryleigh, I think I do," Kaci said. Then she added with a chuckle, "And now I think I need to hear what Dad and Mom are supporting now."

Travis walked over and slipped his arm around his wife's waist. Grinning, he said, "It appears Mike's offhanded comment about Ryleigh's Rescue will become a reality."

"Oh?" Meghan said, feigning surprise.

Ryleigh walked up, put her arm around her mom's shoulder, and grinned. "Well, you see, it all began with a dog…"

Meghan shook her head and said, "I seem to remember a baby bird."

With that, Travis put his arms around two of his favorite women and roared in laughter as they headed toward the kitchen for lunch.

"I can't wait to see Mike's reaction," Meghan said. "He's coming to dinner tonight. You'll have to be sure to tell him what he started."

"It's not Mike's fault, Mom," Ryleigh corrected. "Remember, it all started with a baby bird."

* * *

After polishing off the last of the roast beef and mashed potatoes on his plate, Mike pushed his chair away from the dining room table.

He looked across the table at Ryleigh and grinned. "So, your mom tells me you have something you want to tell me. Or blame on me. I'm not quite sure which. Is this a dining room conversation, or do we need to get comfy out in the living room?"

Travis laughed as he pushed back his chair and stood. "Why don't we all go out to the living room? Honey, I can help you with the dishes later."

As Mike pulled out Meghan's chair for her, he leaned over and gave her a peck on the cheek. "Another fabulous meal, my dear. I don't know why you guys keep feeding me."

"You're family, Mike," Meghan replied, smiling. "Dad always taught me to keep the family fed."

Mike chuckled as he walked toward the living room. Meghan quickly put the leftovers in the refrigerator and then joined her husband on the sofa.

"So…" Mike said with a grin.

"First of all, Mike," Ryleigh began, "you are not to blame in any way!"

Mike looked over at Travis and said, "I'm not sure if that should scare me, or if I should be relieved."

"Do you remember when I first got home, and you found out about my little adventure finding Jack?"

"You mean when you fell off the mountain and blamed it on Sage?" Mike asked playfully.

Ryleigh grinned. "Yeah, that's the one."

Mike nodded and said, "I remember."

"Well," Ryleigh continued. "you said that if I was going to continue rescuing critters, I should hang out my shingle."

"Just to clarify," Mike said with a mischievous grin, "I believe I said you should hang out your shingle if you were going to continue falling off mountains and rescuing critters. I seem to recall there being mention of a mountain."

"Okay, I'll give you that one. I did fall off a mountain. And for the record, you're as bad as JC."

"Thank you," Mike said, grinning. "I'll take that as a compliment."

"Anyway," Ryleigh continued, "I've been thinking about what you said. And I think you're right. Even though I don't have any plans to fall off another mountain anytime soon, I *am* going to continue rescuing animals."

"You don't say," Mike said with interest.

"Yep. I'm going to talk to Aiden and Matt about building a house on my lot next door if you don't have them too busy building houses in your development. But I plan to set aside part of the property, along the back, for an animal rescue operation. And, it will be called Ryleigh's Rescue."

"Ryleigh's Rescue," Mike said, nodding. "I like that."

"You should," Ryleigh laughed. "It was your idea!"

"It was? I must be more clever than I thought! Okay, so tell me a little about your idea."

"Well, I haven't planned it out in detail. I just bounced the idea off Dad and Mom this morning. But I was thinking about having the guys construct a building along the back part of my property that is set up to house several animals. Something similar to the way humane shelters are set up, so each animal has its own space. Then there would be a small kitchen with a sink and refrigerator and a storage area for food and supplies. Oh, and probably a washing station to make it easier to bathe the dogs."

As Ryleigh explained her ideas, Mike had been sitting in his chair nodding his head.

"I think it's a great idea, Ryleigh!" Mike said enthusiastically, sitting on the edge of his chair. "And you know what? I've been looking for another project. I'd be honored if you would allow me to sponsor Ryleigh's Rescue."

Ryleigh looked over at her parents, who simply shrugged, then looked back at Mike.

"Mike, I wasn't looking for you to sponsor my plan," Ryleigh explained. "I just wanted to tell you about it since you planted the idea in my head."

"Oh, I understand that Ryleigh," Mike said. "And I didn't take it that way at all. Your family knows I enjoy helping out with projects that I think are worthy endeavors. It's kind of what I do."

Ryleigh nodded. "I know what you have done, and continue to do, for JC's Hope. You're incredible, Mike."

"I was telling you the truth, Ryleigh. I've been looking for another project, and I think your idea is great. Let's face it. The animal shelters in the area, like most areas, are overcrowded. Far too many animals are put down. If you could set up an operation to rescue some of those animals, restore them to health, and find good homes for them, it would be a win-win situation for Hope."

Ryleigh looked to her parents for advice. Travis and Meghan simply shrugged before Travis finally said, "Ryleigh, if there's one thing I've learned over the past few years, Mike is going to do what Mike is going to do. So, you might as well just nod and thank him."

"Thank you, Mike! Thank you so much! I accept your most generous offer to sponsor Ryleigh's Rescue."

"I just have one small request," Mike said with a grin. "Sage has to be the CRO."

"CRO?" Ryleigh asked, confused.

"Chief Rescue Officer, of course!" Mike laughed.

* * *

Ryleigh stood in the middle of her vacant lot, watching the sun come up. She expected to be joined soon by her dad and mom, as well as Aiden and Matt. She knew the guys were busy at the construction company and building houses in the Hope Estates development. She felt guilty asking for some of their precious time, but they had assured her they were happy to help. Just as she started walking toward the back of the lot, she saw Aiden come out of his house next door and head her way.

"Morning, cuz," Aiden greeted as he hugged Ryleigh.

"Good morning, Aiden. I hope I didn't make you get up too early."

Aiden laughed as he pointed across the lot. "Are you kidding me? As you can see from the group heading our way, I don't think there's a single person in this family who can sleep through a beautiful sunrise."

Ryleigh turned to look behind her. Sure enough, not only were her dad and mom headed toward them, but so were Matt and Emma, followed by JC.

Chuckling as everyone gathered around, Ryleigh said, "I guess I should have brought donuts for this early morning meeting. I didn't expect such a crowd."

Right on cue, Matt's stomach growled, and everyone laughed. "Yeah," Matt said, grinning. "Donuts would have been a good idea."

Emma linked her arm with her husband's and said, "I doubt you're going to go hungry, Matt. Bailey just texted me and said she will be out in a few minutes with hot breakfast burritos for everyone."

"I have the best sister-in-law," Matt said as he rubbed his stomach. "I knew Bailey wouldn't let me starve."

"I swear, Matt," Aiden said, "I used to think JC was a bottomless pit. But I'm pretty sure you could eat him under the table."

"Hey," JC said with mock indignation. "I resent that!"

"How about if you boys have an eating contest later," Ryleigh suggested with a smile. "Let's get this discussion started since most of us need to get to work soon."

Matt was momentarily distracted when he saw Bailey walking toward them with a container of breakfast burritos, but once he had one in his hand, he turned his full attention to Ryleigh.

"First of all," Ryleigh began, "I want you guys to know how much I appreciate your help building the shelter. I know you're very busy down at the shop and building houses for Mike. But I really appreciate your help."

"You should know by now, Ryleigh," Aiden said, "we're always here to help. So, what did you have in mind?"

Leading the group toward the back of the property, Ryleigh pointed toward the back corner. "Somewhere along here, I would like to have you build a basic shelter structure. Nothing fancy. Just a long rectangular building. I'd like it to be set up kind of like other pet shelters, where there are several separate areas for animals."

"How many separate quarters were you thinking for the animals, Ryleigh?" Aiden asked.

"Maybe six or eight," she replied. "I just want to make sure each animal has its own space. I can't imagine I would ever have more than half a dozen animals at a time. I know it's back here at the edge of the property, but do you guys think it would be possible to include a common area for a kitchen? I'd like to have a refrigerator and sink, so that would require plumbing."

"That won't be a problem," Aiden said. "You're going to be having us build a house for you, I assume, so you will be putting in a well and septic system. So, we'll have access to water. I suggest you decide where you want your house located on the lot as soon as you can. Then talk to the parents and they can help you figure out the best location to drill the well and put the septic tank and drain field."

"We can help you with that," Travis said. "That's not a problem."

"What are you planning to do for fencing, Ryleigh?" Matt asked. "Are you just going to have a small fenced area or a larger area?"

"Eventually, I will probably fence the entire back yard area. Maybe with some nice vinyl fencing. But I want chain link fencing to be able to see into the animal area."

Matt looked toward the side of the property. "So, maybe what you do is go ahead and fence the entire back property line with your vinyl fencing, and at least partway up both sides until you're ready to fence the entire back yard. Then you could put chain link fencing and a gate across the front of the shelter. That way, the property is set up to finish fencing the yard, but you'll be able to see into the shelter area and access it easily."

"Thanks, Matt," Ryleigh said. "I think that's a great idea. I'll have Dad and Mom help me come up with some dimensions for the building. And I'm sure Mom would be willing to whip up some blueprints for me. But now I need to let everyone, including me, get to work. Thanks again for everything, you guys."

"Hey Ryleigh," Emma said as the group began breaking up. "You know what I think would look cool? Why don't you have the guys put a nice gable over the front door to the shelter? That way there would be a perfect place to put a sign for Ryleigh's Rescue. And it would give it a little character instead of just being a plain rectangular building."

Ryleigh smiled. "That's perfect, Emma! I'll have them do that!"

Running to catch up to her mom, dad, and brother, Ryleigh beamed with excitement as she took JC by the arm. "This is so great, JC. You're rescuing troubled teens, and I'm rescuing abandoned animals. God is good!"

"All the time, Ry," JC said as he embraced his sister. "All the time."

Chapter Ten

Summers were historically busy for construction families, and it was no different at Byers Construction. The addition of Phoenix Rising Homes to the business meant things were frequently hectic, with multiple projects going on simultaneously. Besides running the construction company, Aiden and Matt continued building houses in the new development in town owned by R & M Development. However, taking a cue from their hard-working father who founded Byers Construction, Todd and Meghan always insisted on putting family first. They were not to allow work to take away from family time. A balance was necessary to preserve everyone's sanity.

The celebration of Aiden and Bailey's and Matt and Emma's first anniversaries had prompted a family barbecue not long after Ryleigh moved back to Hope. Another gathering would be in a few days to celebrate Levi's second birthday. Wyatt and Spencer would be riding over from Seattle with their parents for the family event. Joseph Campbell had been hearing his sons talk about the animal rescue operation Ryleigh was setting up, and he was very interested to see how that was going.

Ryleigh looked out across her property to where the well drillers were setting up their rig to begin drilling. She chuckled to herself when she saw that both her dad and Uncle Todd were already there talking to the men.

As she walked their way, Sage and Jack fell in behind her, always ready for an adventure. She turned and looked at the two dogs and knelt in front of them.

Taking Sage's little face in her hands, Ryleigh looked into her eyes. "Okay, you two. You can come with me, but you have to listen to me and stay back. If you don't listen, you both will be going right back home. Do you understand?"

Sage wagged her tail, then looked at Jack.

"Got it, Jack?" Ryleigh said. "That means you too. You have to listen to me, or you'll be going back home."

With both dogs wagging their tails, the trio started across the field.

Approaching her dad and uncle, Ryleigh smiled and said, "Why am I not surprised you two are already out here supervising?"

Todd hung his head, feigning shame, and said, "I'm sorry, Ryleigh. It's in my DNA. I just can't stay away from a construction site."

Ryleigh laughed. "Don't feel bad, Uncle Todd. My parents aren't any better. But a girl shouldn't complain about having two top-notch supervisors in her corner, right?" Glancing over at the drilling crew, Ryleigh said, "I assume you have them all squared away?"

"Yeah," Travis replied. "The drilling should be starting before long."

"Can you guys come over toward the back of the property with me for a minute?" Ryleigh asked. "I wanted to bounce a couple of ideas off you. Mike and I were talking the other night, and I think he had a great idea that I hadn't thought about. I wanted to get your opinion before I have the fencing guys come out."

As Ryleigh started walking away from the drilling operation, Travis looked over at the dogs, who had been sitting obediently a few yards away. "Well, come on, you two. You don't want to miss anything."

Yipping and barking, Jack and Sage ran ahead of the group, happy to be included.

Pointing along the back property line, Ryleigh said, "I definitely want to put up vinyl fencing along the entire back line, then start up the other side far enough to get past where the chain link fencing will begin. Originally, I was going to come up the side along the access road with vinyl as well. Mike suggested maybe leaving a small area just off the road for a couple of parking spaces. I hadn't thought about that, but it makes sense. As he pointed out, that would eliminate people having to traipse in and out of my back yard. What do you guys think?"

Travis nodded in agreement as he said, "I agree with Mike. I think that's a good idea. That would separate the rescue operation from your house and yard."

"Yeah," said Todd, nodding. "It would also provide a dedicated entrance for Ryleigh's Rescue. Good idea."

"Okay, thanks," Ryleigh said. "Then I'll plan to use chain link fencing along the parking area and the front of the shelter. That should still provide plenty of outside play area for the animals."

"With a gate off the parking area and one into your back yard," Travis suggested. "That would also make parking and unloading pet food and supplies a lot easier. You're allotting nearly a quarter of an acre for the rescue operation, Ryleigh. I think that will give you plenty of room."

The three started walking back toward Ryleigh's parent's house, with the two dogs leading the way down the access road.

Looking at her dad, Ryleigh asked, "Is everything ready for Levi's birthday party this weekend?"

"You would have to ask Amy to be sure," Travis said. "But when I talked to your brother last night, it sounded like they had things under control." Turning to Todd, he asked, "Did Nicole find out if she has this weekend off?"

"She's working on it," Todd replied. "The ER schedule shows her on call this weekend, but she's pretty sure she'll be able to find someone to cover for her. She loves her work, but will be glad when she retires and can stop missing out on family events."

"I know how she feels," Ryleigh said. "That's the way I always felt when I was away at college. I can't believe that little guy is going to be two already. And Amy is pregnant again! I hope she and JC have a little girl. We need to even out the odds around here or the boys will take over!"

"I don't know," Todd laughed. "Sophie has no problem holding her own with the boys."

"Agreed," Travis laughed. "You don't have to worry about Sophie. She's just like her mother!"

"And her grandma!" Ryleigh added with a chuckle. "The girls in this family are tough!"

Sage barked in solidarity, then ran toward the house.

* * *

After a successful birthday party where two-year-old Levi spent as much time playing with the dogs as he did with his new gifts and his cousins, everyone began working their way toward the back of the property. Even though the actual construction had not begun, everyone was excited to hear about Ryleigh's plans for the rescue operation.

Aaron and Sophie were racing Levi down the access road toward Ryleigh's property. Running and barking alongside the kids were two very happy dogs. Sage and Jack loved it when the entire family gathered. They were guaranteed to have adventures and lots of playtime with the kids. The adults strolled down the road, happy to let the kids run off some energy. With several pairs of adult eyes trained on the kids and the dogs, they weren't worried about anyone getting into trouble.

Spence took Ryleigh by the hand and began walking toward the drilling rig. He and Wyatt were every bit as excited about the construction activity as the kids were. The well had been dug and capped off, but the drilling rig was still parked off to the side.

"Now that the well is dug," Spence said, "when is construction on the building going to start?"

Aiden and Matt walked up beside Spence, and Matt pointed to some stakes pounded into the ground several yards away.

"The location of the building, and a few other things, are already staked out," Matt said. "I think we're going to get a crew started on the building next week. Isn't that what we decided, Aiden?"

"Yeah," Aiden agreed. "It really won't take long to put up the building. It's going to be pretty basic."

Joseph Campbell followed Travis and Todd to the very back of the property where the stakes were located. They were soon joined by Mike, Wyatt, and several other family members, all wandering around the area, checking things out.

"Hey, Spence," Joseph yelled across the field to his son, "why don't you guys join us over here so Ryleigh can tell us about her project?"

Once the rather large group had assembled near the stakes in the ground, Ryleigh began explaining her plans.

Chuckling, Ryleigh said, "I didn't expect this to generate so much interest." Turning to JC and Amy, she said, "Sorry about this. I didn't mean to infringe on Levi's birthday."

JC looked off in the distance where the three kids were playing. "Oh, yeah," he said with a laugh, "he looks concerned that he's not the center of attention."

Amy added, "He would rather be running around outside with the dogs and his cousins anyway. Keeping that little tornado inside has become a real chore now that he's more mobile."

Vicki reached over and squeezed her daughter's hand. "That little boy sure loves those dogs. And it's great that his cousins are close, so he has other kids to play with. I still can't believe my grandson is two already!"

Mike walked over and put his arm around Ryleigh's shoulder. "Besides, your rescue operation gives us something to do between the birthday celebration and the afternoon barbecue. Tell everyone your plans."

"Well," Ryleigh began, "most of the family who live here in town have heard all of this. But I know this is the first time Mr. and Mrs. Campbell have been over since this started."

"Can I interrupt you for just a minute, Ryleigh?" Joseph asked. "I know I've mentioned this before, but we've been part of this family for over a year now. Let's dispense with the formalities. Please, call us Joe and Hannah."

"You're right, Joe," Ryleigh said with a smile. "I'll try to remember that.

"I'm sure Wyatt and Spencer have probably told you a little bit about what I'm planning. Especially after the excitement we had on our last trip over from Seattle. Anyway, I have this lot that's just shy of one and a quarter acres. I'm going to dedicate this back quarter acre to the rescue operation. Aiden and Matt are getting ready to construct the building that will house the animals. It's going to have several separate areas for the animals, as well as a kitchen, storage area, and bathing station."

"I assume you must be planning to have a fenced area, so the animals have some outside time as well?" Joe asked.

"Absolutely," Ryleigh replied. "As Mike pointed out when he first unknowingly planted this idea in my head, all the area shelters are overcrowded, and they are forced to put down a lot of animals. If we can help save some of those animals, I want to do that. I've already contacted our local shelter and discussed my plans with them. They are currently several animals over their capacity. Knowing this operation won't take long to get up and running, they plan to hold off on euthanizing for the time being, so I can take some of those animals off their hands. Once an animal comes to my shelter, the plan is to have them checked out by our local veterinarian, give them whatever vaccinations are needed, restore them to good health, and then rehome them."

"This is a great thing you're doing, Ryleigh," Hannah Campbell said, nodding. "Spencer has told us so much about the gift you have with animals."

Meghan walked over to her daughter and said, "Ryleigh has been rescuing animals her entire life. Now she's just making it official. And it will be nice for her to have a dedicated space for it."

"How can we help?" Joe asked.

Ryleigh looked at her dad and mom and shrugged her shoulders.

"You know," Meghan said, "if anyone wants to help with some of the physical labor to get the shelter up and running, that will free up Aiden and Matt for some of their other projects. I know Bailey and Emma loved it when they helped out on Josh and Amy's house."

Looking over at Aiden, Meghan asked, "What do you think? Getting help with painting the building inside and out, maybe even helping with Sheetrock and siding?"

"I think that's a great idea!" Aiden replied. "Our crew can construct the building, then we could schedule a weekend work party for whoever wants to help with the finish work. I have no doubt Bailey would want to help."

"Count me in!" Spence said.

"Me too!" Wyatt added.

"When you get to that point, Ryleigh," Joe said, "let Spence know and all four of us will plan to drive over from Seattle for the weekend to help. I think it would be great to get away from the computer for a while and do some honest work with my hands."

"If Aiden and Matt don't have me scheduled to work on one of the houses in the development when you have that work party," John began, "I'd love to help too."

"Since I'm usually not on the road for work on weekends," Jason said, "I'd like to help. Work keeps me out of town a lot during the week, so I tend to miss out on the fun stuff."

Ryleigh smiled as she looked at her family. "Wow. This is going to be a lot of fun! And we'll make it a family affair. That way everyone can be part of Ryleigh's Rescue. You guys are great!"

About that time, Matt raised his hand, grinned, and said, "Did someone mention something about a barbecue?"

Mike looked at his watch and said, "It's two o'clock. How did you guys ever plan mealtimes before Matt came around?"

Emma reached over and took her husband by the arm. "Come on, Matt. You can lead the way. I believe it's your turn to man one of the grills."

Mike walked up beside Matt and said, "Pretty clever, Matt. If you're doing the cooking, you can decide when we eat!"

"Exactly!" Matt said as he took off running toward JC and Amy's house.

Chapter Eleven

Travis and Todd were back in their element when they joined the crew to construct the building for Ryleigh's Rescue. As anticipated, the building went up quickly. While everyone coordinated their schedules for a weekend work party, Todd and Travis insisted on laying the roofing shingles so the boys could focus on their other projects. By the time the volunteers arrived, the building had been erected, roofing laid, and doors hung. Off to the side of the building, stacks of siding and Sheetrock had been delivered.

Typical for her family, there was already a small group of workers on the jobsite before the sun had risen over the horizon. Since Aiden and Matt were currently working on finishing two new houses in the development in town, they turned over the supervision of Ryleigh's project to Travis and Todd. Spencer and his family had arrived in town last night, anxious to join the others for the weekend project.

Once all the volunteers had assembled on the property, Ryleigh addressed the group.

"I want to thank all of you in advance for your willingness to help," Ryleigh said, smiling. "It's going to be an exhausting weekend, but I think it will also be a lot of fun. For those of us who have known Mike Slater for a few years, we already know that one of the things he likes to do is order pizza to be delivered from Luigi's whenever we have a building project. He has informed me that hasn't changed, so we will all take a lunch break to enjoy pizza on Mike. My mom and Vicki volunteered to watch the kids while we work, so my dad and Uncle Todd will be kind of in charge of this weekend as our other resident construction experts."

Ryleigh added with a chuckle, "Oh, and since Aunt Nicole knows her husband so well, even though she's on duty at the ER this weekend, she said she'll be available in case someone decides to fall off the roof. Or, and I quote, 'one of the other silly things boys tend to do.' And now I'll let Dad and Uncle Todd take over and explain their plans."

Todd looked around the group and said, "First of all, I want to set the record straight. I do *not* make a habit of falling off roofs."

Meghan cleared her throat and said, "Uh…"

"Okay," Todd laughed. "So, I fall off one little roof and I'm scarred for life?"

"Well, actually, little brother…" Meghan smiled. "I don't think that scar in the middle of your back is going anywhere."

"Aren't sisters great?" Todd said as he hugged Meghan. "Anyway…back to the business at hand. I know Emma and Bailey have some experience putting up siding and painting. Joe, have you or your boys ever done any of this stuff before?"

"Actually, we have," Joe said, nodding. "It's been several years, but when I had the dairy farm, we usually did whatever needed to be done. So, I've hung some drywall and installed siding. I'm a fair painter. Wyatt and Spence used to be fairly handy installing siding, so I'm sure they could help with that. Right, boys?"

"Sure," Spence said. "We'll help wherever you need us."

"I want to help too," Hannah added. "I've never done siding or drywall before, but I'm a quick learner. So, wherever you need an extra set of hands, I'm here to help."

"That's great," Todd said. "This will work out just fine. One of us can manage the crew hanging drywall, and the other can help with the siding. Do you have a preference, Travis?"

"If you don't care," Travis said, "why don't you run the drywall crew and I'll work out here with the siding crew."

"Sounds good," Todd said. "Jason, I know you've done a little of everything over the years – one of the hazards of marrying into this family. Do you want to work on siding or drywall?"

"Either one is fine with me," Jason said. "Drywall tends to require more hands, so I can help out with that if you want."

"Perfect," Todd said. "Ryleigh, you, Emma, Bailey, and Hannah can work with Travis on installing the siding. Wyatt, if you and Spence don't mind getting some drywall experience, you can help Jason, me, and your dad with that. When we break for lunch, we can reassess how the work is progressing and decide if we need to switch up crews and get more people on the drywall. If we can finish most of the siding and drywall today, we should be able to devote tomorrow to painting the outside of the building. We'll probably have more people to help out with that. JC said several of the teens from the youth center have offered to come help paint tomorrow. The interior painting will be done later, since we'll need to tape and texture in there before we paint."

"Well," Travis said as he put on his gloves, "are we ready to get to work?"

"Oh," Ryleigh added, "I almost forgot. Mom has a cooler inside already stocked with water and other cold drinks, so help yourselves."

* * *

The morning flew by with tremendous progress made both inside and outside the building. Just before lunchtime, Mike Slater pulled his pickup onto the property and three teenage boys climbed out with him. They grabbed boxes of pizzas and bags of garlic bread and headed toward the building.

Travis laughed as he walked toward them and said, "What's this, Mike? Did you honestly think we need reinforcements to help eat pizza?"

Mike laughed. "No, but I did bring reinforcements. These three boys were hanging out at the center and wanted to come help with the project. Two of them are in Todd's apprenticeship program down at the shop, so they've had a little drywall experience, and hope to get some more hands-on experience."

About that time, Todd walked out of the building, dusting off his jeans.

"Hey, Devin," Todd said, shaking hands with the teens. "I didn't know you and Jake were coming over."

Shaking hands with the third boy, Todd introduced himself. "Hi, I'm Todd."

The young boy was about fifteen years old and promptly reached his hand out to Todd. "I'm Chase. I've heard Devin and Jake talk about the apprenticeship program you have. I just started taking the woodshop class at the high school and was hoping I might be able to join your program. Either way, the three of us are here to help this afternoon."

"That's great!" Todd said. "We can use some help hanging drywall. The siding crew is getting ahead of us, and we can't have that!"

Travis signaled to the others working on the siding. "Mike's here with lunch, so let's take a break, and we can regroup after lunch."

Turning to the older boy, Mike said, "Devin, why don't you grab that folding table from the back of the truck and set it up in the shade near the building? We can put the food on that."

"You got it, Mike," Devin replied, as he headed toward the truck.

Within a few minutes, everyone had filled their plates and grabbed a cold drink to settle in for a much-needed break.

Immediately after lunch, everyone got back to work. Todd was thrilled to have the extra help hanging drywall. By the time the weary crew called it a day, all the siding had been installed and most of the drywall was ready to be taped and textured. Everyone gathered just outside the main door to the building to make a game plan for the following day.

Todd walked up behind Chase and put his arm around the young boy's shoulder. "You're a quick learner, Chase, and a hard worker. I would love to have you join the apprenticeship program at Byers Construction. Talk to your shop teacher and have him give me a call and we can work out the details."

Chase beamed with pride. "Thanks, Todd! You won't be sorry, I promise."

"Jake and Devin," Todd began, "I'm sure glad you boys showed up to help this afternoon. The four of us were making pretty good progress, but having the extra hands made a world of difference. Thanks."

"We had fun, Todd," Jake said.

"Well, Travis," Todd said, "what are your thoughts for tomorrow?"

Looking around the outside of the building, Travis said, "We just have one small area to finish adding the trim, otherwise the outside is ready to be painted. And there's just one little area of drywall to finish before we can tape and texture. Joe, do you and your boys think you can finish up the last of the drywall in the morning?"

"Not a problem," Joe replied. "I think we can finish it in about an hour."

"If they work on finishing the drywall, Todd," Travis said, "you and I can begin taping and texturing. That way we can have everyone else work on painting the exterior of the building. It should go pretty fast with that many hands."

"Okay, sounds good," Todd agreed.

Looking at the three teenagers, Todd asked, "Are you boys planning to come back tomorrow?"

"Sure!" Devin and Jake replied simultaneously.

"You bet!" said Chase.

"Do you boys need rides in the morning?" Travis asked.

"I'm going to run them all home now," Mike said. "I can pick them up in the morning and bring them over."

"Thanks, Mike," Travis said. "Thanks again for your help, boys. We really appreciate it. Hey, wait a minute. Can you guys call home and see if it's okay to stick around for dinner? I happen to know Meghan has cooked up several pans of enchiladas she's keeping warm in the oven. You boys are welcome to join us for dinner if you get the okay from your parents. We can make sure you get rides home afterward."

After a few hasty phone calls, everyone headed toward Travis and Meghan's house to wash up and enjoy a well-earned dinner.

* * *

Once things settled down for the evening, and everyone had a chance to get cleaned up, most of the family gathered on Matt and

Emma's back deck to relax and visit. Joe and Hannah were enjoying time with their daughters and being away from the fast pace of the city.

Sitting beside his wife on one of the loveseats on the deck, Joe tipped his head back and closed his eyes momentarily.

"You know," Joe said, "sometimes I miss the slower pace of country life. Everything in the city is so rushed. You don't have a chance to sit back and simply breathe in the fresh air."

Travis glanced over at Joe and said, "That fresh air is even more relaxing after a hard day of work like we all put in today."

Joe sat up, placed his elbows on his knees, and rested his chin in his hands. "That's something else I realized tonight. Working with your hands, doing physical labor, that's a different kind of exhaustion than working on a computer all day. I miss that."

Travis chuckled and said, "Let's see how you feel at the end of the weekend. You may be ready to sit back down at your computer."

Joe laughed and said, "You could be right. But I'm looking forward to finishing the drywall in the morning and maybe helping you guys out with the taping and texturing. And I'm on board for coming back over to help with the rest of the painting. Assuming the workaholics in your family haven't finished it by next weekend."

"Speaking on behalf of the workaholics," Ryleigh said, smiling, "I make no promises."

Once again, Joe had tipped his head back and closed his eyes. Speaking with his eyes closed, he said, "Now that those tasty enchiladas have had a chance to settle, do you know what sounds good right now? A big ice cream sundae. Maybe I'll make a quick run into town and grab some ice cream for everyone."

Matt had barely jumped up from his chair when Emma joined him. "Before Matt says anything, Dad, we have a better idea. Why don't we all go into The Creamery for ice cream?"

The young adults were instantly on their feet.

Wyatt was quick to look at his older sister and say, "That's right! Bailey still owes me and Spence a trip to The Creamery."

Meghan chuckled as she joined the others already standing. "Wyatt, why don't you save that and collect on it another time? Tonight, the ice cream is on us. As a thank you for all your hard work this weekend."

Aiden walked over to Matt and said, "Well, buddy, it looks like we're on our own for ice cream since we weren't part of today's work party."

"As long as I get ice cream," Matt said with a grin, "I don't really care who pays for it!"

Meghan playfully slapped Matt on the arm and said, "Come on, boys. The ice cream is on us tonight. After all, we wouldn't be having this work party if you boys hadn't constructed the building. Besides, the weekend isn't over. We may find a paintbrush tomorrow that fits your hand!"

* * *

By the end of the weekend, the crew of volunteers was exhausted but happy with the progress they had made. The building looked great. The exterior was finished except for the addition of a custom-made sign to be installed above the door. Travis and Todd planned to finish the last of the texturing and hook up the plumbing in the kitchen in the next few days. Joe and his family were excited to return next weekend to help paint the interior of the building.

After getting cleaned up and packed, everyone gathered on Matt and Emma's back deck before Joe's family drove back to Seattle.

"You know, Travis," Joe said, "this has been one of the most satisfying weekends I've had in a long time. It's nice to work with my hands again. Thanks for allowing us to come over and help out."

Travis patted Joe on the back and chuckled. "I'm glad we could help you out. But seriously, we're the ones who need to be thanking you. As they say, many hands make light work. You and your family made the work enjoyable. And it was nice to be able to spend time with you. You and Hannah have raised four great kids. They're all hard workers. You should be proud of them."

"Oh, we are," Hannah said. "And we can't wait to come back next weekend to help with the rest of the painting. I honestly had a lot of fun."

"Well," Joe began, "we better hit the road. We have a long drive ahead of us."

Looking around, he asked, "Where did we lose Spence?"

"I think he and Ryleigh are down at the rescue building," Wyatt said.

Joe chuckled and said, "Go corral your brother so we can get on the road."

Wyatt started up the access road toward Ryleigh's property just as Spence and Ryleigh began heading toward him, hand in hand. He continued down the road and met up with them.

"Haven't you gotten tired of my little brother yet?" Wyatt asked Ryleigh with a grin.

"Not yet," Ryleigh chuckled. "Maybe after next weekend," she added, squeezing Spence's hand.

"Dad sent me to corral you, Spence. He's ready to hit the road."

"Okay," Spence replied. "Since we're coming back next weekend, I wish I had brought my laptop over. I could have stayed at Emma's this week and worked from here."

"Yeah," Wyatt agreed. "I was thinking the same thing. Maybe when we come over next weekend, we bring our laptops just in case we want to stay over."

As they stepped onto the deck the boys overheard their dad say, "I wish I had brought my laptop with me. It would be nice to stay here this week since we'll be back in a few days."

Spence and Wyatt looked at each other and laughed.

"Anytime you guys want some fresh air to breathe," Travis said, smiling, "come on over. We promise not to put you to work every time."

"We may take you up on that offer," Joe said as he shook hands with Travis. "This weekend has been an eye-opener."

Chapter Twelve

Juggling multiple projects was such a normal part of life in Ryleigh's family that no one was surprised when Meghan mentioned over dinner one night that the plans for Ryleigh's house were complete. Even though she was retired, Meghan still enjoyed doing design work and creating blueprints. However, she did manage to confine her work to projects for family and friends. She was thrilled when Ryleigh asked her to design her new house and had been working on the plans while the rescue building was being constructed. So, by the time the crew was installing fencing around the rescue property, the foundation was being dug for Ryleigh's future home.

Spence had made it a habit to make the trip from Seattle to Hope nearly every weekend. Sometimes Wyatt rode along with him, and often their parents came as well to spend time with their daughters. Spence stepped off Aiden and Bailey's front porch and began walking toward the Harmon house to meet up with Ryleigh. Out of habit, he looked toward Ryleigh's property and saw her standing in front of the rescue building. Seeing her always put a smile on his face.

"I didn't expect to see you down here quite this early," Spence said as he walked up to Ryleigh. "I was just getting ready to walk up to your parents' house."

Ryleigh stood with her hands in the back pockets of her jeans and was staring up at the gable above the front door.

"My sign is finished, and they'll be delivering it this morning," Ryleigh explained with a smile. "Dad said he'll help me install it as soon as it arrives."

Spence put his arm around Ryleigh's waist and looked from the rescue building to the freshly poured foundation for her new home.

He chuckled as he shook his head. "Does your family ever take a break from projects? You're working on getting the rescue operation ready to open at the same time you're having a house built. And Aiden and Matt will be building your house while also building homes in that development in town."

Ryleigh looked at Spence and smiled as she shrugged her shoulders. "We like to stay busy."

"Apparently," Spence laughed.

Hearing a vehicle, they turned to see Travis walking up the road with a pickup not far behind. The pickup stopped beside him, and Travis pointed toward the rescue building.

"That has to be my sign!" Ryleigh squealed as she started toward the road.

Before long, the sign had been dropped off, and Travis had two ladders leaning against the front of the building.

"This won't take long," Travis said. "Ryleigh, do you want to help me hang the sign, or should Spence help me so you can stand back and watch it go up?"

"Oh, Spence, do you mind helping Dad? I would love to watch the sign be put in place."

"Not a problem," Spence agreed as he started up one of the ladders.

Once the sign had been securely attached to the front of the building, Travis and Spence climbed down the ladders just as Mike Slater pulled onto the property.

Mike got out of his truck and walked over to stand beside Ryleigh. Putting his arm around her shoulder, he nodded and said, "The sign looks great, Ryleigh!"

"Thanks! I agree!"

Travis and Spence joined the others admiring the new sign designating the building as Ryleigh's Rescue.

Looking around the property, Mike said, "It looks like the fencing is complete too. You appear to be ready to open for business!"

"Yeah," Ryleigh said. "They finished the fencing yesterday. And the sign is installed now, so I guess you're right. I must be ready to open for business."

"Well, in that case," Mike said, "you're going to need what I have in the back of my truck."

Ryleigh and Spence looked over at Travis, who simply shrugged his shoulders. "It's Mike," Travis laughed. "Who knows what he has in the back of his truck."

Everyone followed Mike over to his truck. Ryleigh looked in the back and then looked at Mike in confusion.

"A quad, Mike?" Ryleigh asked. "Is that what you're talking about?"

Mike grinned and said, "A quad would come in handy running up and down the road between your parents' place and Ryleigh's Rescue."

"But I'll eventually be living in my own house just right over there," Ryleigh said, pointing toward her future home.

"Well, you never know when it will be handy for hauling things around the property," Mike reasoned. "Besides, eventually the kids will enjoy riding it around."

"Even the big kids?" Spence asked hopefully.

Mike laughed. "Even the big kids, Spence. In fact, I took it for a little spin before I brought it over this morning. And I would just bet Sage would love to ride on it."

Ryleigh shook her head. "You are unbelievable, Mike. What are we going to do with you?"

"Just feed me occasionally," Mike laughed. "Now, Travis and Spence, why don't you help me unload this toy? Uh, I mean this much-needed piece of equipment."

As soon as the quad was unloaded, Ryleigh said, "I almost forgot. I have the animal beds and food and water dishes in my car. Since I appear to be ready for business, I need to run up to the house and bring my car back."

Mike pointed at the quad and said, "See, it's coming in handy already."

Spence was practically dancing with excitement. "Ryleigh, can I take you to get your car?"

Ryleigh laughed. "Boys and their toys! Yes, Spence, you can take me to get my car. But I'm driving the quad back. I'm going to see if Sage wants to ride back with me. You can drive my car."

"It's a deal," Spence said, wasting no time climbing on the quad. He patted the seat behind him and said, "Climb on, Ryleigh! Let's go for a ride!"

Spence and Ryleigh took off down the road on the quad, leaving Travis and Mike standing in the middle of the road shaking their heads and smiling. Before long, they heard the sound of the quad and watched as it circled the corner in front of JC and Amy's house and started back up the access road.

Ryleigh was slowly leading the way up the road. Sage was standing in front of her on the quad, with her two front feet firmly planted on the handlebars, yipping into the wind. Jack was running alongside the quad, barking, happy to be included in another adventure. Spence followed a safe distance behind in Ryleigh's car. After parking the quad, Ryleigh picked up Sage and placed her on the ground. She immediately began running around the quad, trying to jump back onto the seat.

Travis laughed at the puppy's antics and said, "You may have started something. Now she's going to want to ride on the quad all the time."

Sage had her front feet on the footrest of the quad, looked at Ryleigh, and yipped. She was obviously ready to go for another ride!

Ryleigh stood with her hands on her hips, staring at the puppy, and said, "You could be right, Dad. Can you imagine what it will be like when Aaron and Sophie start riding the quad? Sage will never want to walk anywhere!"

* * *

Spence and Travis helped Ryleigh set up the animal beds and dishes inside the rescue building while Mike made a run to the pet store for supplies. By the time they were finished, there were eight separate living areas for rescue animals. Mike returned with several bags of dry dog and cat food, canned food, vitamins, and animal treats. He had also purchased several pet leashes, flea collars, and other necessities to stock the pantry.

Looking around the building, Ryleigh said, "Well, guys, do you think I'm ready to go?"

"Everything looks great, Ryleigh," Travis said.

Mike added, "If you find out you need something we didn't think of, just let me know and I'll get it taken care of. When are you going to contact the animal shelter in town?"

"They called me yesterday," Ryleigh said. "They have two dogs right now that have been there for quite a while, and they're out of room. They said I could stop by any time to pick them up."

Mike looked at Spence and asked, "Well, Spence, are you ready to get your feet wet in the animal rescue business? If Ryleigh is ready, we can take my truck and go get those dogs right now."

"You bet!" Spence said. "I can't wait to see how this all works."

"Really, Mike?" Ryleigh asked. "Dad, can you come with us?"

"I wouldn't miss it!" Travis replied. "You need to take Sage and Jack home anyway, so we can take my truck."

"Grab a couple of those leashes, Ryleigh," Mike suggested.

"Since I'm the only one who hasn't had a chance to ride the quad yet," Travis said, "I get to drive it back to the house. Climb on behind me, Ryleigh."

As soon as Ryleigh got on the quad, Sage began yipping.

Travis patted the seat in front of him and said, "Well, come on, Sage. Jump up here and we'll go for a short ride."

With Sage looking out over the handlebars and Jack running alongside, they started up the road. After a quick stop at the house, the group was on their way to pick up the first two residents of Ryleigh's Rescue.

* * *

Spence was curled up on the floor in the corner of one of the rescue building's pet areas, holding a terrified older dog. The small brown and white female terrier mix was one of two dogs they brought back from the local shelter. She had been scheduled to be put down. Someone dropped her off at the shelter a few months ago with a note attached to her collar. The note simply said her name was Coco and her owner could no longer care for her.

"How can someone just drop off this sweet dog?" Spence asked Ryleigh when she finished getting the second dog settled into his space. "Old dogs at shelters don't stand much chance of finding homes. Everyone wants the cute little puppies."

Ryleigh sat down beside Spence and patted the top of the old dog's head. "You're right, Spence. Most people who go to shelters for pets want cute little puppies and kittens. But there's a good home out there somewhere for Coco. And she will stay here until we find that home."

"Did you get Duke settled in?" Spence asked, referring to the bulldog they brought in.

"Yeah, he just curled up on his bed and fell asleep."

Pointing to the dog in Spence's lap, Ryleigh added, "Speaking of sleep, it looks like Coco has calmed down. Her eyes are drooping."

"How can you rescue animals and not want to keep every single one of them?" Spence asked honestly.

Having overheard Spence's question as he walked up, Travis chuckled. "Believe me, it was a constant battle, Spence! We did keep a fair amount of her rescued animals, but Ryleigh, and the rest of the family, got pretty good at finding homes for them. And you notice that Sage and Jack didn't go anywhere. Don't worry about Coco. She's a sweet old girl, and I have no doubt Ryleigh will find the perfect home for her. In the meantime, you can give her lots of attention when you're in town. You have the same soft heart for animals that Ryleigh has."

"I think when I come over next weekend, I'm going to bring my laptop and plan to stay for a week and work from Emma's house," Spence said, stroking the now-sleeping dog on his lap. "If you have time, Ryleigh, maybe we can go up to the lake you're always talking about."

"That's a great idea, Spence!" Ryleigh replied. "Things have been so busy getting the rescue operation up and running, getting started on building my house, and work being chaotic. Taking some time off and doing something fun will be a nice change."

Spence looked at Ryleigh and smiled. "Who knows? Maybe Coco would like to go on an adventure with us."

Travis laughed as he headed toward the door. "Surrender, Spence. She's got you hooked."

"Who? Coco or Ryleigh?" Spence asked, smiling.

Travis smiled and shrugged his shoulders as he walked out the door.

Chapter Thirteen

Spence and Ryleigh had packed a cooler with drinks and food for their trip up to Paradise Lake. They had planned to make a day of it and take a much-needed break. They gathered food and water dishes and a leash for Coco, who seemed eager to go on an outing. The old dog had been settling in nicely at Ryleigh's shelter and was becoming more social. Spence played a huge part in Coco's beginning to relax and feel at home. Whenever he walked into the shelter, Coco rewarded him with a wagging tail and an occasional bark.

Ryleigh's entire family was supportive of her rescue operation. Family members always stopped by to check on the animals, take them for walks, and see if any new animals had been brought in. Aaron, Sophie, and little Levi were always anxious to spend time with the dogs, and Sophie frequently asked if any kittens had joined the shelter. Ryleigh's Rescue had truly become a family affair. The family's involvement made it easier for Ryleigh to take an occasional break, and she was looking forward to spending the day with Spence at the lake.

Spence walked out of the shelter grinning, with Coco tucked under his arm, and met Ryleigh at her car.

"I think we got everything," Spence said, patting Coco on the head.

Ryleigh grinned and said, "I'm not sure who's more excited to go to the lake, you or Coco."

"Of course, she's excited," Spence said. "This is her first adventure in who knows how long. I think she'll have a great time."

"Well," Ryleigh said, "I'm sure glad you didn't want to bring Duke, Sage, and Jack along too!"

"Don't be silly, Ryleigh," Spence laughed as he settled Coco in the back seat. "There's not room for everyone in your car. You may need to get a bigger car someday."

Ryleigh laughed. "Just get in the car, Spence."

The drive up to Paradise Lake was always relaxing for Ryleigh. With the river meandering alongside the road in several places, the view was magnificent, and it provided many opportunities to stop along the road to enjoy the river and the scenery.

Before long, Ryleigh pulled into a parking space at Paradise Lake. Coco was anxious to get out of the car, so Spence attached her leash and sat her down on the gravel.

"We can leave the cooler in the trunk for now," Ryleigh said. "Let's walk around for a while until we get hungry. I'm sure Coco is ready to do some exploring."

With Coco's leash wrapped around one wrist, and Ryleigh's hand in his other hand, Spence was all smiles as they started down the path toward the lake. Ryleigh welcomed the relaxing stroll through the pine trees and could instantly feel the pent-up tension leave her body. Coco seemed fascinated by the chipmunks who frequently ran across the path, and occasionally gave a little yip at them.

As soon as they stepped out of the trees and Spence caught his first glimpse of the lake, he dropped Ryleigh's hand and started down toward the water. Ryleigh smiled as she slowly followed behind him, with Coco bravely leading the way. Once they reached the water, Coco tentatively put one foot into the lake's edge, then looked back at Spence. She made no move to walk out into the water but did get a small drink from the lake.

When Ryleigh stepped up beside Spence, he looked at her and said, "It's so peaceful. Now I understand why you couldn't live in the city."

Ryleigh pointed across the water to a small island in the middle of the lake. "Do you see those people fishing from the bank of that island?"

Spence looked in the direction she was pointing and said, "Wow, I never even noticed them there."

"All the kids in our family grew up fishing off that bank, including my cousin Aiden. But even with people fishing out here, it's still peaceful and quiet. I love this place."

"I can see why," Spence said, gazing across the lake.

"Do you want to sit over here on the grass along the bank for a while?" Ryleigh asked.

"Sure. Lead the way."

Ryleigh took Spence's hand and walked a hundred yards or so down the bank to a grassy spot. Coco curled up between them on the grass and promptly fell asleep.

"I think Coco likes it here too," Spence said, petting the old dog.

After watching someone on the island catch a fish, Spence said, "That fish makes me think of food. Are you getting hungry? I can go get the cooler if you want."

"Do you want us to come with you, or do you want to come back here to eat?" Ryleigh asked.

"This is a great spot for a picnic," Spence replied. "You can wait here with Coco, and I'll be right back."

"Okay," Ryleigh said, smiling. "Don't let the chipmunks get you."

As he started back down the trail, Ryleigh could hear Spence chuckle. "Yep, I'll make a country boy out of him yet."

* * *

After the most relaxing day either of them had had in a long time, they decided it was time to head back to town. Ryleigh picked up Coco's leash and started to stand. Spence helped her up, then pulled her into a gentle hug. Stepping back, he removed her sunglasses and placed them on her head.

Looking her in the eyes, Spence said, "Thanks for bringing me up here, Ryleigh, and showing me your world."

Not breaking eye contact, Ryleigh replied, "It's the least I could do. You showed me your world."

"I think I like your world better," Spence said quietly. Then he leaned down and placed a tender kiss on her lips.

With her eyes closed, Ryleigh whispered, "I like my world better too."

In the middle of their second kiss, Coco began jumping on their legs, trying to get their attention. They both looked down at the dog simultaneously and nearly bumped heads. Spence reached down, picked her up, and held her so they were face to face.

"We need to come to an understanding, girl," he said in mock seriousness. "If you're going to come on adventures with us, you need to work *with* me. No more interrupting kisses. Got it?"

Coco wagged her tail and barked in agreement.

"Now that we have an agreement," Ryleigh chuckled, "let's head back. We'll have time to stop along the river for a few minutes."

Spence leaned down to set Coco back on the ground and gave Ryleigh a quick peck on the cheek on the way back up. When Coco barked, they both laughed, then the three headed for the car.

About forty-five minutes into their drive back to town, Ryleigh pulled the car off onto a wide spot and parked along the river.

"Let's get out for a few minutes, Spence. It's beautiful here. The river is absolutely mesmerizing."

With his arm around Ryleigh's waist, they stood along the riverbank for several minutes, watching the river bounce along the rocks. When Coco started getting antsy at the end of her leash, they decided it was time to go.

As they walked back to the car, Spence noticed an old cardboard box in the brush along the river. Shaking his head, he said, "I don't understand why people think it's okay to toss their trash out along the road. Or along the river."

Handing Coco's leash to Ryleigh, he said, "Here, if you'll take her, I'll go grab that box and throw it in the trunk. We can toss it in the trash when we get back to town."

When Spence leaned over to grab the box, he suddenly hesitated and stood back up. "Uh, Ryleigh, I think you need to come look at this."

Ryleigh walked over beside Spence, and he pointed down at the box. Curled up in a tight ball inside the box were four little kittens. Without hesitation, Spence picked up the box and headed to the car. Ryleigh got Coco settled in on one side of the back seat, and Spence placed the box of abandoned kittens on the other side.

Ryleigh started the car and glanced over at Spence.

Shaking his head, Spence asked, "How can anyone abandon a litter of kittens in a box along the river? Did they think tucking them back into the bushes so they wouldn't be seen easily would make them feel better about it?"

"I don't know, Spence," Ryleigh said honestly. "But out of all the places along the river where we could have stopped, God directed us to this spot. And He made sure you saw the box. I can't explain why people do the things they do. But I know these four little ones will have a place at Ryleigh's Rescue until we can find permanent homes for them."

Spence suddenly smiled and said, "Well, that'll make Sophie happy!"

* * *

Once they were back on the road, Ryleigh called Kevin Draper and talked to him about the kittens. He was getting ready to head past their house to check on an animal a few miles from town. He said he would drop off some kitten formula for them and then stop by in the morning to check them over.

The remainder of the ride back to town was quiet. Even though they had had a relaxing day, Ryleigh could tell Spence was disturbed by finding the abandoned kittens.

She reached over and placed her hand on his forearm. "Animals are abandoned more often than people realize, Spence. That's why animal shelters are so important. You grew up on a dairy farm in the country before you moved to the city. Were animals ever dumped off at the dairy farm?"

Spence looked into the back seat at the box of kittens. "You know, I honestly don't know. There were always cats around. It was a given. I always thought it was because it was a dairy farm, and cats were just part of life."

"You should ask your dad," Ryleigh said. "I would bet some of those cats were dumped off at the farm."

"You're probably right."

When Ryleigh parked the car at the rescue center, Spence looked over at her and pointed to the building. "This is a good thing you're doing, Ryleigh."

Ryleigh pointed to the box in the back seat and said, "And that was a good thing you did today, Spence."

As they were getting out of the car, they heard the quad and saw Travis coming up the road toward them. He parked the quad next to Ryleigh's car and climbed off.

Handing them a bag, Travis said, "Kevin dropped off some kitten formula and small bottles for you a few minutes ago. He said you would explain."

Ryleigh smiled and looked at Spence. "Do you want to field that question, Spence?"

"Well, Travis," Spence began with a smile, "it all started with a cardboard box."

Travis held up his hand and laughed. "Enough said. I'm going to assume you have a cardboard box with kittens in the car. And fair warning, the kids were at the house when Kevin dropped that off. Sophie's first question was, why do you need kitten formula, Papa? I told her she would have to ask Aunt Ryleigh. So, you can probably expect to see them down here soon."

"Give us a few minutes to get the kittens settled into one of the spaces inside, Dad, then the kids can come down to see them. Maybe they can help us feed them."

"Okay," Travis replied. "By the way, Mike will probably be down too. He's at the house and is concerned about Coco being missing. He didn't know she was going on an adventure with you two today. He thought maybe you had found a home for her. Did you know he's been coming by every day to see her?"

Ryleigh smiled and nodded. "I was pretty sure I had seen him popping in frequently. I thought he was just checking supplies. I should have known he was visiting Coco. She always seems excited to see him. I'm going to put her back in her room. Tell Mike to come on down."

While Ryleigh got Coco settled in, Spence brought in the box of kittens and set it on the floor in the common area. Ryleigh chose one of the spaces at the end of the room where it would be quieter for the kittens. By the time they had transferred the kittens from the cardboard box to their new bed, Spence heard a vehicle pull up outside. Moments later, Mike walked into the building, followed by Aaron and Sophie.

Mike went directly to Coco's room, picked her up, and looked her in the eyes.

"So, Miss Coco," Mike said seriously, "I understand you went on an adventure today."

Coco wagged her tail and licked his cheek.

"Why don't you tell me all about it?" Mike said as he sat in one of the chairs along the wall and patted the old dog's head.

In the meantime, the kids quietly walked over to the room with the kittens and knelt beside their bed.

"Would you kids like to help us feed the kittens?" Ryleigh asked.

The twins nodded simultaneously, without saying a word.

Before long, Ryleigh, Spence, Sophie, and Aaron each had a kitten in their lap and were feeding them with a bottle. Ryleigh looked up and met Mike's eyes. Coco was asleep on his lap, and he was gently petting her. He nodded at Ryleigh and smiled.

When Ryleigh finished feeding her kitten, she sat him down in the pet bed and walked over to sit beside Mike. She reached out and stroked Coco.

"You can take her home whenever you're ready, Mike. This sweet girl belongs with you."

Chapter Fourteen

After the rescue operation was up and running, construction began on Ryleigh's house. Since both Travis and Todd were now retired, and neither of them could stand not having a project to work on, they were leading the crew on Ryleigh's house. Aiden and Matt checked in frequently to see how things were going, but had mostly turned the project over to their mentors.

Spence had been watching the progress on the house during his weekend visits to Hope. He told his parents how amazed he was at how fast the house was being built. After getting a taste of working with his hands again, Joe Campbell decided it was time to call Travis.

Once they exchanged greetings on the phone, Joe got down to the purpose of his call. "You know, Travis, helping out on building Ryleigh's Rescue rekindled a spark in me. After becoming entrenched in the technology industry, I had forgotten how much I enjoyed working with my hands. And, of course, being in Hope had the added benefits of spending time with our daughters and enjoying the peace and quiet of the country."

"It's a different lifestyle than the fast pace of the city, Joe," Travis said.

"I have some vacation time wasting away," Joe continued. "If I take a week off to visit the girls, what are my chances that you and Todd would let me help you at Ryleigh's house?"

Travis chuckled. "You caught the construction bug, didn't you, Joe? It's easy to see why. It's satisfying work. And I have always loved watching a pile of building materials be transformed into something beautiful and useful."

"I seem to remember the girls telling me you used to build custom homes," Joe said.

"I did," Travis confirmed. "I loved building homes. That's why I tried to stay connected to construction even after I joined the ministry. Now that I'm retired, and the boys are busy building houses in town, Todd and I are like little boys in a toy store being able to build Ryleigh's house."

"Yeah, I bet," Joe said. "So, what do you say? Can you guys use a week of free labor?"

"Come on over, Joe. Are Hannah and the boys coming too?"

Joe laughed. "Hannah is sitting beside me with her bag packed and her fingers crossed. And you already know I can't seem to keep Spencer home these days. Wyatt is always game. He and Bailey like to keep score on who owes who lunch or ice cream from The Creamery."

"In that case, Joe," Travis said, "load up the family and come on over. If Bailey and Emma don't have room for all of you at their houses for the week, Meghan and I have plenty of room here."

* * *

Two days into his week-long vacation, Joe seemed to always have a smile on his face. Todd and Travis welcomed the extra help on the house and chuckled every time they had difficulty convincing

Joe to take a break. Since Bailey and Emma worked during the day, Hannah enjoyed helping the guys. She didn't seem to care if she was helping carry plywood or refilling their nail pouches. She was happy to be involved. And everyone marveled at the progress on the house.

Todd and Joe climbed down from the roof and Spence met them at the bottom of the ladder.

"Hey, Dad," Spence said as Wyatt walked up beside him. "Wyatt and I want to know if we can help with the shingles. I know we've never done roofing before, but we'd like to learn."

"You're going to have to ask Todd," Joe replied, smiling. "He's in charge of the roofing."

Spence looked at Todd and said, "How about it, Todd? Are you willing to teach a couple of techies how to lay shingles?"

Todd pulled his gloves off and shoved them in his back pocket. He looked from the boys to the roof, back to the boys, then grinned.

"I don't see why not," Todd said. Looking down the road at an approaching pickup, Todd added, "That looks like Mike bringing pizza for lunch. How about we get you two up on the roof right after lunch and see how things go."

Wyatt and Spence grinned and gave each other a high-five.

"Thanks, Todd!" Wyatt said. "I promise, we're quick learners."

Todd patted Wyatt on the back and said, "I've already figured that out, guys. Now let's go get some of that pizza before Travis eats it all."

Mike parked his truck in front of the house, then reached over and unhooked Coco's seatbelt. As soon as he sat her on the ground, she ran over to Spence and begged to be picked up.

Mike looked at her and laughed. "Are you trying to convince Spence you don't get enough attention from me?"

Spence picked up the old dog and held her up to his face, grinning. "You know what I think, Miss Coco? I think you're a drama queen. Running around acting like you don't get any attention. I'm pretty sure you go everywhere with Mike these days. I don't think I've seen him without you since the day he took you home."

Coco licked Spence's cheek, then scrambled out of his arms to follow Mike as he carried pizza to the makeshift table.

As soon as everyone finished lunch, Wyatt and Spencer tossed their plates into the trash bin and then hurried over to the ladder leaning up against the house.

"We're ready whenever you are, Todd," Spence said.

Todd laughed as he tossed his paper plate into the trash. "Okay, boys, head on up the ladder and we'll get you some hands-on training laying shingles."

"Do you want me back on the roof too, Todd?" Joe asked.

"Yeah, come on up," Todd replied. "Once we show them the ropes, you can work with one of the boys and I'll work with the other."

"Todd," Travis said, "did you say the windows will be delivered this afternoon or tomorrow?"

"Aiden said they'll be here first thing in the morning."

"Okay." Turning to Hannah, Travis asked, "Well, Hannah, how would you like to help me run some electrical wire this afternoon? Unless you'd rather take a break and hang out with Meghan and the kids. Meghan loves construction, but I think she loves being a grandma even more!"

"I'm sure she does!" Hannah said. "I can't wait to be a grandma. But, in the meantime, let's run some electrical wire!

* * *

Just as the work crew gathered tools, ready to call it a day, Aaron and Sophie ran up the road toward Ryleigh's place. They headed straight into the rescue building to visit the animals. Less than a minute later, Aaron ran back out the door with one of the baby kittens in his arms.

"We forgot something," Aaron said to no one in particular. "Grandma said dinner is ready, so everybody's supposed to go up to the house."

Travis reached over and tousled the hair of his oldest grandson. "So, seeing the kittens was more important than telling us about dinner?"

Aaron grinned and said, "Papa, we can eat anytime. How often do we get to see the kittens?"

"Pretty much every day, buddy," Travis said with a chuckle. "Why don't you and Sophie make sure the kittens are back in their room, then you can ride up to the house with me."

"Okay, Papa. We want to talk to you about something anyway."

As he passed Todd on his way to put the kitten back in its room, Aaron said, "Oh, Uncle Todd, I forgot to tell you something."

Todd laughed. "Your memory seems to be running on empty today, buddy. What were you supposed to tell me?"

"Aunt Nicole said not to eat without her. She's on her way to Grandma's house now." Not waiting for a reply, Aaron turned and ran back to the rescue building to return the kitten to its room.

While Todd helped Joe and the boys put away the last of the tools at Ryleigh's house, Travis made sure all the animals were in their rooms and the rescue building was locked.

Travis climbed into his truck beside his grandkids, started the engine, and then asked, "So, what did you two want to talk to me about?"

Sophie looked at her brother and said, "You tell him, Aaron."

Aaron looked at his grandpa hopefully. "Papa, will you help us talk Mama into letting us have one of the kittens?"

Travis grinned but didn't reply immediately.

"Please, Papa," Sophie pleaded.

"Are Mama and Daddy at the house?" Travis asked.

"Yes," Sophie said. "They're helping Grandma with dinner. Will you talk to them with us, Papa?"

"Have you already asked them about the kittens?" Travis asked.

The twins nodded simultaneously but said nothing.

"And what did they say?"

"Daddy said it was up to Mama," Aaron said.

"And Mama said she would think about it," Sophie added.

"So, they didn't say no. Is that right?" Travis asked, to clarify.

"No, they definitely did not say no," Aaron said emphatically.

Travis grinned as he pulled into his driveway. "Okay, I'll see if I can help you out."

"Thanks, Papa!" both kids yelled as they scampered out of his truck and ran towards the house.

All through dinner the twins glanced at their grandpa, hoping he wouldn't forget to talk to their mom about the kitten. They even loitered in the kitchen while the food was put away, then offered to help load dishes into the dishwasher. Once everything was tidied in the kitchen, everyone moved to the living room to relax and visit. Somehow Aaron even convinced Levi to sit with them on the floor for a few minutes, promising to play with him soon.

Travis had been watching the kids, knowing they were bursting with anticipation. He winked at them, then glanced at Kaci and Jason.

Speaking to no one in particular, Travis said, "Ryleigh tells me the kittens are doing well. It will probably be time to find homes for them soon."

Not realizing Travis was leading up to something, Spence unwittingly helped him out.

"Yeah, probably," Spence said. "It will be hard to see them go. It's so hard not to get attached to the rescue animals."

Looking at his oldest daughter, Travis said, "You know, Kaci, a kitten could be good for the kids. They've been helping Ryleigh and Spence care for them since the first day they brought them home."

Kaci grinned and said, "I see it didn't take those two long to get Papa on their side."

Travis laughed. "What can I say? I have very persuasive grandkids."

Kaci looked at her two kids, trying to hide the fact that she had already decided about the kitten.

"A kitten is a big responsibility. It's not just another toy for you to play with until you get tired of it. It requires care and attention, even if you have other things you'd rather do."

"We know, Mama," Aaron said hopefully. "Sophie and I have been helping Aunt Ryleigh take care of them."

"We even fed them with bottles until they were big enough to eat kitty food," Sophie added.

"I don't know, kids," Kaci said. "It's hard to take a little kitten away from his littermates."

Aaron and Sophie looked at each other, put their heads together, then began whispering.

"We have a great idea, Mama," Sophie said. "Why don't we take two kittens? That way, Aaron and I can both have a kitten, and they can play together."

"They won't be sad that way because they will have one of their brothers or sisters with them," Aaron added diplomatically.

Kaci looked at her husband, and Jason simply shrugged and smiled.

"Okay," Kaci said. "You can each have a kitten. But you can't take them home until Aunt Ryleigh tells you they are ready to leave the shelter."

The kids jumped up and hugged their mom and dad, then gave Travis an extra big hug.

"Thanks, Papa!"

In their excitement, Sophie suddenly stopped and announced, "Mama, we need to go to the pet store. The kittens need a bed and kitty food and flea collars and toys."

"And don't forget they will also need a litter box and kitty litter," Kaci said, grinning.

Aaron wrinkled his nose and said, "Oh, yeah. I guess it's a good thing they're cute!"

Travis laughed, then said, "Well, that leaves two more kittens."

Looking at JC and Amy, he said, "Hmm, there's Levi, and another baby on the way. I believe that adds up to two kids and two kittens."

JC held up his hand in protest. "Don't even go there, Dad. Sage and Jack already spend as much time at our house as they do here. Levi thinks Jack is his dog. We don't need kittens too!"

Ryleigh looked around the room and said, "Don't worry, Dad. We have a big family. And I'm pretty sure I'll be able to keep the entire family supplied with animals."

Meghan glanced at Mike and said with a chuckle, "See what you started, Mike?"

Cuddling Coco in his lap, Mike laughed and said, "It seems to me I remember hearing that it all started with a bird. That was before my time!" Petting the top of Coco's head, he added, "Besides, I already did my part."

Chapter Fifteen

While work continued on Ryleigh's house, the rescue operation was in full swing. Word had spread around town about the new animal shelter, so it was common for people to bring abandoned animals by, knowing they would be taken care of and rehomed. Ryleigh continued working with the other local shelter to take in any animal that was scheduled to be put down. And Mike ensured the vet bills for all the animals were taken care of.

Things had been going so well at the shelter that Ryleigh's Rescue was always at or near capacity. When she rescued Sage from the side of the road, she had no idea how busy she would become with animals. Even though there were days she wasn't sure if she was coming or going, she was happy. And far too busy. It was time to recruit some help because she had no plans of ever turning away an animal who needed her.

Kaci and Jason stopped by Travis and Meghan's house to pick up the twins. Ryleigh had called Kaci earlier in the day and said she wanted to talk to her and Jason. The kids ran in from the family room as soon as their parents arrived.

"Do we have to go home already, Daddy?" Aaron asked.

Jason laughed. "You've been here all afternoon. Don't you think Papa and Grandma are tired of you yet?"

Sophie giggled. "Daddy, Grandma and Papa would never get tired of us."

Meghan hugged her only granddaughter and said, "You're right, sweetie. You two can stay a little longer. You've been inside playing for a while. Go out and run around the yard with Sage and Jack for a few minutes while we talk to Aunt Ryleigh."

As the twins bounced off the back deck, Ryleigh chuckled and said, "Oh, to have the energy of an eleven-year-old!" Turning to Kaci and Jason, she added, "All that excess energy is exactly what I want to talk to you guys about."

Kaci nudged her husband and said, "Oh, good. I thought she was going to give us the other two kittens!"

Jason smiled and said, "What's up, Ryleigh? And before you ask, no, I haven't figured out how to bottle that energy. If I did, I certainly wouldn't still be working!"

Ryleigh laughed as she sat down on the sofa beside her parents.

"As you guys have noticed, the rescue operation has gotten very busy," Ryleigh began. "And I seem to be running myself ragged. I didn't want to mention this to the kids unless I had cleared it with you, but would you have any objections if I hired Aaron and Sophie to help out at the shelter?"

Jason looked at his wife and shrugged. "What did you have in mind?"

"I thought they could help feed the animals and make sure they all had some outside time. Maybe sweeping out the cubicles and generally helping to keep the building tidy. And it would give them some spending money."

"I think it's a great idea, Ryleigh," Kaci said. "They already spend a lot of time down there, and they love helping with the animals. Honestly, they would probably do all those things without being paid."

Travis laughed and said, "That's what I told her."

"I would feel better about it if I paid them for their work," Ryleigh said.

Kaci looked at her husband, and Jason nodded. "It's fine by us."

Meghan opened the sliding door and yelled into the back yard. "Come on, kids, it's about time to go home."

The kids ran through the house and headed toward the front door.

Travis caught Aaron as he ran by. "Slow down there, buddy. Aunt Ryleigh wants to talk to you two before you leave."

Once she had their attention, Ryleigh asked, "How would you two like to work at the shelter with me? I need help feeding the animals, giving them outside time, and cleaning their cubicles. That kind of thing. I was thinking about hiring you to help out."

"But, Aunt Ryleigh," Sophie said, "we already help you do some of that stuff."

Aaron held up his hand. "Wait a minute. Are you saying you want to *pay* us to do those things?"

"Sure. What do you say?"

"But we like doing those things, Aunt Ryleigh," Aaron said. "You don't have to pay us."

Ryleigh sighed. "You two are the best kids ever. But I'm still going to pay you. That means you'll need to do everything I ask you to do to help out, okay?"

"You're going to pay us to hang out with the animals?" Aaron asked once again, shaking his head. "I hope you know, Aunt Ryleigh, we would've done it for ice cream."

Meghan laughed at the honesty of her grandson, then watched as the twins whispered back and forth.

Aaron nodded at Sophie, then turned to Ryleigh. "Okay, Aunt Ryleigh, you've got a deal. On one condition. We'll keep doing the stuff we already do, and whatever else you need us to do. You can pay us. Then we're going to donate our pay to Ryleigh's Rescue."

"Come here, you two," Ryleigh said, pulling the twins into a hug. "You two are unbelievable. I love you both so much."

Aaron took his sister by the hand, and they headed to the door. Sophie whispered into Aaron's ear, he grinned, then said, "But we wouldn't turn down ice cream either!"

* * *

Ryleigh was scrambling to finish a project before another presentation with her boss in Seattle. The shelter had been occupying so much of her time lately that she frequently found herself working on design projects well into the evening. Her self-imposed goal was to get this project finished by lunchtime. She was closing in on her goal by mid-morning when her cell phone rang.

Glancing over at her phone, the caller ID indicated her sister was calling.

"Hey, Kaci," Ryleigh said. "What's up? You're at work, aren't you?"

"Hi Ryleigh," Kaci sighed. "Yes, I'm at work. And I know you're trying to finish that project, so I really hate to bother you. But I have a problem, and I'm afraid you're the only one who can help me."

"It's no bother, sis. I always have time for you. What do you need?"

"There's a dog that's been hanging around the shop here for the past couple of days. It looks lost, but won't let anyone near it. I don't think it's abandoned because it appears to be well cared for. It's one of those dogs with the long flowing hair. We've been putting out food and water, but it still won't let any of us get near it. I know you're really busy, Ryleigh, but is there a chance you can come check it out? If anyone can get near it, it would be you."

"It sounds like an Afghan Hound," Ryleigh said. "Those are beautiful dogs, but they're high maintenance because their hair requires pretty much daily brushing. So, you're probably right about it being lost, rather than abandoned. Give me five minutes, then I'll head over."

"I'm really sorry, Ryleigh," Kaci said. "But I'm afraid it could get hurt hanging around here with all the trucks and forklifts running around."

"It's really not a problem, Kaci," Ryleigh said. "I'll be over in a few minutes and check it out."

Ryleigh met her sister in front of the Byers Construction office twenty minutes later. Kaci led her around to the far side of the shop and pointed to a dog lying in the shade alongside the building.

"What do you say, Ryleigh?" Kaci asked. "Do you think you can work your animal whisperer magic?"

Ryleigh smiled as she slowly walked toward the dog. "I guess we'll find out in a minute."

As Ryleigh approached the dog, it picked up its head and looked at her, but didn't appear frightened. She moved slowly, talking softly, soothingly, and soon found herself within a few feet of the dog. She quietly sat on the ground, bringing herself to the dog's level. Glancing back at her sister, Ryleigh was surprised to find several people standing beside Kaci, watching.

"You're a beautiful dog," Ryleigh said. "I'm not going to hurt you. I'm here to help. That's a pretty collar you're wearing. I'll just bet you have some jewelry on it that might tell me your name."

Ryleigh patted the ground beside her and asked, "Would you like to come over and show me your jewelry?"

The dog looked around and seemed to decide Ryleigh was safe. So, it got up and walked over to sit beside her.

Ryleigh began petting the dog's head while she reached for the collar. "I'm glad to see you have a tag on. Let's see what your name is. Ginger, huh? Well, Ginger, you're a beautiful girl. Oh, good, your tag has a phone number for your parents. Shall I give them a call, girl? I bet they really miss you."

Kaci, Aiden, and several employees had been watching Ryleigh work her magic from across the parking lot. The dog who wouldn't let anyone near it all week was suddenly lying beside Ryleigh resting its head in her lap.

"I swear that girl has always been an animal whisperer," Kaci said, shaking her head in admiration.

A few minutes later, Ryleigh and the dog walked up to the group in the parking lot.

"Hey, everyone," Ryleigh began, "this sweet girl is Ginger, and she's been lost for nearly a week. I just talked to her owners. They came through town several days ago and stopped at the park, where Ginger gave them the slip. She likes to play Houdini occasionally, and she's been known to travel quite a ways, so they've been frantically searching for her. I'll take her home with me and keep her at the shelter. They'll come pick her up tomorrow."

Once Ryleigh had gained Ginger's confidence, she allowed the others to pet her. She wagged her tail and seemed happy to find a new bunch of friends.

Kaci hugged her sister and said, "Thanks so much, Ryleigh. I knew you would be able to help. Sometimes you truly amaze me."

"Thank you guys for putting out food and water for her," Ryleigh said. "That way she didn't have to wander around town and maybe end up getting hurt."

Reaching down to pet the dog, Ryleigh said, "Well, Ginger, let's get you to your B & B for the night. Mom and Dad will be here to pick you up tomorrow, and it sounds like you'll be getting another lecture about playing Houdini. You really need to find another hobby, girl!"

Ginger wagged her tail happily and followed the animal whisperer to her car.

* * *

After doing some fast shuffling around at the shelter, Ryleigh was able to make room for their overnight guest. Aaron and Sophie were a big help and instantly fell in love with the long-haired dog. When Kaci and Jason stopped by to pick up the kids at the end of the day, they walked in to find Ginger had drawn quite a crowd. Travis and Meghan were there, along with several other family members. Mike rushed over with Coco as soon as he heard about the Afghan, and Coco quickly befriended Ginger. Sophie became Ginger's self-appointed groomer and followed her around with a brush so she could take care of any sudden tangles.

Standing back and watching everyone's reaction to the newest guest, Ryleigh shook her head as she looked around the shelter.

"I need more room," Ryleigh said to no one in particular.

Jason walked up beside his sister-in-law and chuckled. "Have you resorted to talking to yourself now?"

Ryleigh laughed. "I guess I have, Jason. I was just saying, apparently to myself, that I need more room. I'm always at capacity. I don't have room for any more animals, but I won't turn any away. I might have to look at expanding the shelter."

Jason folded his arms across his chest as he surveyed the room. "Expanding could certainly be an option, Ryleigh. But you wouldn't need to expand if you could rehome some of these animals."

"You're right, of course. And I've been working on that. But people don't just pop out of the woodwork."

By now, Kaci had joined her husband and sister and was listening to the conversation.

"How about promoting the shelter with an event of some type to draw people in?" Jason suggested. "Maybe Adopt A Pet Days?"

"Oh, Jason, that's a great idea!" Kaci said as she grabbed her husband's arm. "You know, Ryleigh, something like when Josh had the career fair at JC's Hope. An event to show people their options. I bet you'd have a great turnout."

"Wow! I've been so busy running the shelter that I never thought about something like that," Ryleigh said. "I hope Aaron and Sophie won't regret agreeing to work with me here, because I'm going to need a lot of help."

"Trust me, Ryleigh," Jason said with a chuckle, "they'll love it. You'll be lucky if you can get rid of them. Maybe I should bring their sleeping bags over and they can camp out with the dogs."

Ryleigh laughed as she playfully slapped her brother-in-law's arm. "I think I need to go rescue Ginger, otherwise your daughter is going to brush all her hair out before her owners get here tomorrow!"

Chapter Sixteen

Ginger's owners, Alex and Stacy Moreland, stopped by the following day to pick up their lost dog. They were impressed with Ryleigh's Rescue and showed their gratitude by donating to the shelter. After spending nearly an hour visiting and checking out the animals, Ryleigh told them about her plans to have an Adopt A Pet event soon.

"That's a wonderful idea, Ryleigh!" Alex said. "We're a couple of hours away, but we'd love to come back and check it out if you let us know when it's going to be."

"I'd be willing to bet some of our friends might come too," Stacy added. "Mark was saying just the other day that he wants to find a small dog for his mom. And I saw a couple that might be perfect for her."

"That would be fantastic!" Ryleigh said excitedly. "I need to go to Seattle for work tomorrow. But once I get back I'm going to start planning it. I have your contact information, so I'll be sure to text you when I've decided on the dates."

"Well, come on, Ginger," Alex said, smiling. "We need to get this escape artist out of here before she disappears again."

Shaking Ryleigh's hand, Alex added, "Thanks again, Ryleigh. Ginger couldn't have found a better retreat."

Kneeling beside the Afghan, Ryleigh looked her in the eyes and said, "You be good now, Ginger. No more disappearing acts, okay?"

Ginger wagged her tail, licked Ryleigh's cheek, then pranced to the door, ready to leave on her own terms.

* * *

Somehow, despite all the distractions at the shelter, Ryleigh managed to finish her work project before the scheduled presentation in Seattle. She and Spence had been so busy that they hadn't spent much time together. Since she would be going to Seattle anyway, they decided to meet up to have an early dinner at one of his favorite restaurants.

After another successful presentation, Ryleigh's boss walked her down to her car. Samantha knew about Ryleigh's passion for animals and was aware she had set up an animal shelter. Ryleigh told her boss about the overcrowding situation at the shelter and her plans to schedule an Adopt A Pet event.

"I think you would be able to find homes for a lot of your animals with an event like that," Sam said, "and it sounds like fun! With your design talent, I have no doubt you'll do a great job promoting both the event and Ryleigh's Rescue. Get your name out there and let people know you exist. Then I bet you wouldn't have to worry about overcrowding."

"You're right, Sam," Ryleigh nodded. "That's a good idea. I could put something together without much trouble."

"When do you think you'll have the event?" Sam asked.

"Maybe in a couple of weeks. I don't think it'll take long to organize, and my entire family is willing to help."

"You let me know when you plan to have it, Ryleigh, and maybe I'll make a trip over to Hope. It sounds like my kind of town, and I'd love to meet your family. Now get out of here so you're not late for your dinner date. Tell Spence I said hello."

* * *

Ryleigh was so thankful for her supportive family. She knew in her heart that there was no way she would be able to pull off a four-day event without their help. She'd put together an eye-catching ad campaign and word had gotten out around town. Aaron and Sophie had worked hard and did a fantastic job cleaning the cubicles and making sure all the dogs were freshly bathed for the long weekend event. She had already treated them to ice cream, with a promise of more ice cream once things settled down.

Amy and Matt's mom Vicki volunteered at JC's Hope most days but offered to help with Adopt A Pet Days all four days. As soon as Ryleigh's Aunt Nicole learned of her plans, she also offered to help, so Ryleigh made a point to schedule the event during Nicole's four-day-off stretch at the hospital to take advantage of the generous offer. The entire Campbell clan drove over from Seattle, saying they wouldn't dream of missing the event.

Everyone gathered in front of Ryleigh's Rescue, anticipating a large turnout.

Todd walked over and put his arm around his niece's shoulder. "Everything looks great, kiddo. And from the scuttlebutt I've heard around town, I think we're going to be busy. Hopefully, there will still be a few animals left by the last day."

"Wouldn't that be great if we're able to find homes for all the animals?" Ryleigh asked.

Spence took Ryleigh's hand and said, "I know that's the goal. That's the whole point of Ryleigh's Rescue. But, man, seeing all these animals leave won't be easy. It's hard not to get attached to them."

"Unfortunately, Spence," Ryleigh said, squeezing his hand, "there will always be more animals who need to be rescued."

Travis walked over to his youngest daughter and smiled. Pointing down the road, he said, "I hope you're ready, kiddo. Here comes a string of cars."

Things got busy quickly as people showed up for Adopt A Pet Days. Many people from around the area, and even a few who lived right in Hope, mentioned never having heard of Ryleigh's Rescue. Everyone thanked them for helping rescue animals, aware of the overcrowding problem in shelters that forced far too many animals to be put down. Most people who came to check out the shelter left donations, even if they had not intended to adopt a pet.

Aaron and Sophie were leading dogs around on leashes out in the yard, hoping to attract new owners. Before long, Spence and Wyatt joined them with other dogs. The fenced yard in front of the shelter became a parade ground. Kids from some of the families who showed up for the event asked if they could walk the dogs. Aaron was very serious as he showed the younger kids how to handle the animals.

Partway through the event's second day, the main shelter in town called Ryleigh to ask if she could take a few more animals. They were over capacity once again and hoped they wouldn't have to put any of the animals down. Not wanting to take Ryleigh away from the shelter, Travis and Todd drove over to pick up the animals.

After showing Vicki what to do with one of the new animals, Ryleigh went back outside. As she looked around, she saw her boss wandering around the yard.

"Hey, Sam," Ryleigh said, walking up to her boss. "I'm glad you were able to come over. Did you just get here?"

"About five minutes ago," Samantha said, looking around. "It looks like you have a good turnout, Ryleigh. I'd love to see your operation. If it's okay, I can just wander around. Or, if you happen to have a few minutes, maybe you can show me how you have the inside of the building set up to house the animals."

"The whole family is here helping, Sam," Ryleigh said, smiling. "I don't know what I'd do without them. So, I can take a few minutes to show you around."

"I'm in town for the night," Sam said, "so I'd love to meet your family at some point."

As they walked toward the building, Ryleigh waved her arm theatrically and said, "Welcome to Ryleigh's Rescue! Come on in."

Ryleigh gave Samantha the grand tour, such as it was, of the inside of the facility.

"This is impressive, Ryleigh," Samantha said, nodding. "You've created a good setup for the animals. It's nice to see they aren't just shoved into cages."

"I could never do that, Sam," Ryleigh said, shaking her head. "I try to give them a comfortable home until we're able to find forever families for them."

After looking around and seeing some of the animals inside the shelter, Samantha said, "I'm just going to wander around for a bit and check out the animals if that's okay. The kids have been pestering me for a kitten, and I see you have a couple of litters back there. I purposely didn't bring them with me this weekend, or we would've gone home with a carload of animals! This way, there's a chance I may get out of here with just one!"

Before walking back outside, Samantha slipped a hundred-dollar bill into the donation can.

"Oh, Ryleigh," Samantha began, "I noticed a place in town called Luigi's. Are you familiar with it?"

Ryleigh laughed. "I'm pretty sure my family has sent several of their kids to college with what we've spent there! Best pizza place in town."

"Check with your family, and if you don't already have plans tonight, maybe we can meet up for dinner."

"That sounds great, Sam. I'll check with Dad and Mom and let you know," Ryleigh said.

The afternoon flew by with a fairly steady stream of visitors. As Ryleigh started back toward the building, she spotted a familiar dog out of the corner of her eye.

"Ginger!" Ryleigh said happily as she hurried over to Alex and Stacy and knelt down to hug the Afghan. "Have you been a good girl, Ginger? No more lectures, I assume?"

Stacy laughed as Ginger got reacquainted with Ryleigh. "I told you we'd be back."

"And this time, we're not letting Ginger off her leash even for a minute!" Alex laughed. "Oh, and we brought our friend Mark."

"Hi, Ryleigh," Mark said, shaking her hand. "Alex and Stacy told me about your operation here. It sounds fantastic. I'm hoping to get lucky and find a dog for my mother."

"Have a look around, Mark," Ryleigh said. "Maybe we have the perfect fur baby for your mom. Make yourselves at home. If you have any questions, I'll be floating around somewhere. It's been a couple of busy days!"

Before the end of the day, Mark had found the perfect dog for his mother, an older Yorkie with a mild temperament.

Cradling the dog in his arms, he said, "I think Mom will love her. The only problem is that poor Ruby will get spoiled."

"That's not a bad thing," Spence chuckled. "All fur babies deserve to be spoiled. An older gentleman, a friend of Ryleigh's family, adopted a sweet girl from here. Mike takes Coco everywhere with him. She's probably the most pampered pooch I've ever seen!"

"Every dog's dream," Alex said. "I know Mark's mom, and I'm sure Ruby will be spoiled rotten in no time!"

* * *

Later that evening, after an exhausting day, Ryleigh's family took a break and met Samantha at Luigi's for dinner. Travis called ahead and reserved their large banquet room since several family members had decided to join them. Mike said he planned to join them as well, and he chuckled when Travis added a condition.

"Mike," Travis began, "you know you're always welcome. However, tonight you can come only if you promise to leave your wallet at home."

Mike feigned innocence and said, "But I need my wallet to drive."

Unwilling to be outwitted by Mike, Travis countered, "No you don't, because I'm going to stop by to pick you up! See you at seven o'clock, Mr. Slater!"

Samantha got to know Ryleigh's family over a relaxing dinner and fell in love with Levi, who was a little younger than her kids.

"I drove around a little this afternoon," Samantha said. "This is a charming town, and the perfect size, in my opinion. There are enough shopping options that you don't have to go out of town for every little thing. Yet, it's not so big that you're overrun with people. And you can actually find a place to park!"

"Hope has grown a lot in the past few years," Meghan said, "and it continues to grow. But it's important to the community to maintain that small-town feel. So, I think everyone works hard to do that."

"I think they've succeeded," Samantha said, smiling. Looking at Aaron and Sophie across the table, she added, "And I bet you two would know if there was a good place in town to get ice cream."

"The Creamery!" the twins yelled in unison, causing everyone to laugh.

"Maybe after we finish pizza," Samantha began, "we could all go to The Creamery for ice cream. My treat. That is, of course, if it's okay with your parents."

With praying hands and their best pleading look, Aaron and Sophie silently begged for ice cream.

"How can anyone turn down those adorable faces?" Kaci laughed. "And that, Samantha, is how we ended up with kittens from Ryleigh's Rescue!"

"Speaking of kittens," Samantha said, "I'm going to stop by your shelter in the morning before I head home. Maybe I can get you kids to help me pick out a kitten for my kids."

Aaron and Sophie whispered back and forth, and then Sophie said, "You know, you probably should get two kittens."

Samantha chuckled and asked, "And why should I do that, Sophie?"

"Because then they'll have someone to play with," Sophie said logically. "And they won't be lonely."

"Hmmm," Samantha said as she pretended to consider the thought. "You make good sense, Sophie. Maybe you and Aaron can each pick out a kitten for me. My kids would love having two kittens."

Ryleigh laughed and said, "I think I need to make Aaron and Sophie the ambassadors for Ryleigh's Rescue!"

* * *

The Adopt A Pet Days event was winding down by mid-afternoon of the last day. Not only had Travis and Todd picked up a few animals from the main shelter in Hope, but another overcrowded shelter about thirty miles away also brought in some animals. Ryleigh and her family had done an amazing job finding forever homes for many of the animals. They had decided they probably wouldn't have much more activity, so everyone began gathering things to put back into the building so they could call it a day.

A car pulled into one of the parking spaces at the end of the building and an elderly lady got out and walked into the yard.

"I'm not too late to look at the animals, am I?" the little white-haired lady asked hopefully.

Ryleigh walked over to the lady who appeared to be in her late seventies. "No, ma'am. I'm always willing to show someone our animals."

"Thank you, Ryleigh," the lady said as she reached out to take Ryleigh's hand.

Ryleigh smiled and asked, "How did you know I was Ryleigh?"

The lady chuckled and said, "You don't remember me, do you?"

Ryleigh looked into the woman's face as she dug back into her memory bank.

"You and Josh used to come into our market with your mom when you were little," she said, smiling. "Sometimes Kaci would bring you two in to buy candy and comic books. I never forgot any of the kids who came into the store."

"Grandma Martin?" Ryleigh said tentatively. "Oh my gosh! It *is* you!"

Ryleigh wrapped the elderly lady in a hug, then said, "I remember being so sad when you guys closed your market. I loved your store."

"It was time, my dear," Mrs. Martin said, smiling. "With the big new grocery store opening in town, Herman and I were ready to retire.

"So, tell me, Ryleigh, do you happen to have any small older dogs left in your shelter? After my Herman passed on, the house was just too quiet for my taste. I'd love to find a little dog to grow old with."

Ryleigh linked arms with Grandma Martin and walked toward the shelter. "We still have several kittens, but I think we're down to three dogs. Let's go take a look."

After looking at the remaining dogs, Grandma Martin kept going back to the cubicle that housed an older poodle mix. The small dog seemed frightened and lost and remained huddled in the corner of the cubicle.

"Can I see that little dog, Ryleigh?" Grandma Martin asked.

"Sure. If you'll go over and sit in one of the chairs along the wall, I'll bring her out to you."

A few minutes later, Ryleigh placed the small cream-colored dog in the elderly lady's arms.

"I've had this girl for several weeks," Ryleigh said. "Unfortunately, older dogs are harder to rehome. Peaches is a little more skittish than normal because of all the extra people who've been in and out of the building over the past few days. It's been too much activity for her, and stresses her out."

The elderly lady stroked the dog's back, and she seemed to relax a bit. "I don't blame you for being stressed, Peaches. You're just lying there, minding your own business, and all these people come traipsing through. I think you're a sweet old girl and you need a nice, quiet home. Would you like to come home with me? I promise, there won't be a lot of noisy people wandering in and out. How about if you and I just quietly grow old together?"

Standing off to the side, Ryleigh had been silently watching the exchange when her mom walked in.

Ryleigh put her finger to her lips, then whispered to her mom, "That's Grandma Martin from the old neighborhood market. I think she's going to adopt Peaches."

Grandma Martin stood, holding the little poodle in her arms, and said, "Peaches wants to come live with me, Ryleigh. I think we need each other. And to think I almost decided not to come over. Then, at the last minute, I just got in my car and headed this way."

Putting her hand on the old woman's shoulder, Ryleigh petted Peaches and said, "It appears God was holding Peaches here for you. I think you two will enjoy each other's company."

Peaches was the last animal to be rehomed during the adoption event. Once everything had been put away and the family could take a much-needed break, they gathered on Travis and Meghan's back deck.

"Thank you all for helping out the past several days," Ryleigh said. "I have the best family and I never could have done this without you. We've been going so fast and furiously lately that my brain automatically asked, 'So, what's next?'"

"Ice cream!" Sophie and Aaron yelled.

Ryleigh laughed as she stood and started down the steps. "I think that's the best idea I've heard all day. Come on, everyone. To The Creamery, we go! Treats are on me!"

Chapter Seventeen

Between the rescue operation and house construction, Ryleigh often wondered how she found time to work at her paying job. But she was happier than she had been in several years. She was surrounded by family, she had a satisfying job she loved, and she was rescuing animals. The fact that Spence was now spending more time in Hope than he was in Seattle added to her happiness. She was content.

The entire Campbell clan was back in Hope for the weekend, but no work was being done on Ryleigh's house. After the recent adoption event, everyone was taking some much-needed downtime. Bailey and Emma told their parents about an upcoming concert in their favorite park, so everyone was excited to go. Concerts in the park tended to bring out the entire community, and Ryleigh's family never missed them.

Travis and Meghan arrived with JC, Amy, and Levi and were already setting up lawn chairs under one of the large oak trees in the park. Before long, the rest of the family showed up and began spreading blankets and setting up chairs. With the addition of Matt and Amy's parents, and the Campbells, the large family found themselves sprawling out under three oak trees.

Ryleigh and Spence settled in on one of the blankets near Amy and JC as the bands began tuning their instruments. Spence leaned over and nudged Ryleigh's shoulder as he pointed across the park. Mike was walking toward them with a lawn chair in one hand and Coco on a leash in his other hand.

"Coco couldn't have found a better home," Spence said, smiling. "I'm really glad Mike took her."

"Me too," Ryleigh agreed. "They're good for each other."

"Not long after he got Coco," JC said, "he stopped by the center and asked if it would be okay for him to bring her inside. I laughed and told him he could bring in a camel if he wanted to and I wouldn't stop him! So, whenever he stops by, Coco is with him. Sometimes she wanders around and plays with some of the teenagers, and sometimes she curls up at Mike's feet while he's playing the arcade games."

"He's really something," Ryleigh said.

As Mike approached the group grinning, he asked, "Is this a private party, or can anyone crash?"

"Why don't you come sit with us, Mike?" Matt asked.

Aaron and Sophie jumped up and ran over to Mike.

"Mr. Mike, you need to sit with us," Aaron insisted.

"You kids don't need to hog Mike all the time," Kaci said, laughing. "Let someone else have some time with him."

Mike handed Coco's leash to Sophie and said, "I think I'll go sit with Matt and Aiden and the girls today. Can you take Coco over there while I say hi to everyone else?"

"Sure, Mr. Mike!" Sophie replied happily. "I'll stay right with her until you get there."

"Do you want me to take your chair over for you, Mr. Mike?" Aaron asked hopefully.

"That would be a big help, Aaron," Mike replied, handing him the chair. "Then maybe after a while, we can go check out the food booths."

Mike chuckled at the retreating kids, then walked over to say hi to Travis and the rest of the family.

* * *

Three different bands were scattered around the park playing mostly folk, contemporary, and country music. Joe and Hannah Campbell wandered through the park with Matt and Amy's parents, enjoying each one of the bands. They met up with Bailey and Aiden at the pizza booth.

"Bailey," Hannah said to her daughter, "I'm so glad you told us about this concert so we could come over. The park is beautiful. I can see why you enjoy spending time here."

Bailey reached for her husband's hand and said, "Luckily, Aiden likes the park as much as I do. This is one of our happy places."

Looking around, Joe asked, "Have you guys seen Spence? He was going to show me something called elephant ears."

Bailey laughed and said, "I'm sure he's with Ryleigh, but who knows where that might be. They could be scouring the park for abandoned animals. Now that there's room at her shelter after the adoption event, they're probably working on filling it up again."

"Last time I saw them," Aiden said, "they were headed for the elephant ear booth. It's over that way, just past the hamburger booth. You definitely need to try an elephant ear, whether you find Spence and Ryleigh or not!"

As they approached the elephant ear booth, they found Wyatt standing in line with Matt and Emma.

John Phoenix shook his head as he laughed. "I should have guessed Matt would be in one of the food lines."

"What kind of friend would I be, Dad, if I didn't introduce Wyatt to elephant ears?" Matt said, shrugging his shoulders.

Getting in line behind the others, Joe said, "Spence was going to get one of those ears with me, but I guess we'll grab one with you guys. It's his loss."

Wyatt laughed and said, "Spence didn't miss out on anything. He and Ryleigh have already been through the line. They said they were going to walk around the park and listen to the music."

On the other side of the park, away from the crowded food booths, Spence and Ryleigh strolled hand in hand, listening to the bands.

"Country music is your favorite, isn't it?" Spence asked Ryleigh as they walked toward the small pond in the middle of the park.

"Yes, it is," Ryleigh said, smiling. "How did you know?"

"You always start swaying to the music when it's country."

Ryleigh smiled and said, "It's easy to dance to, and some of it is pretty mellow."

As they approached the pond, Spence pointed to a family of ducks swimming near the shore.

"This is a great park, Ryleigh," Spence said as they walked around the pond. "Even with the loud music playing in the background, it's still relaxing."

They strolled around the pond for several minutes, stopping occasionally when they spotted frogs or baby ducks.

Ryleigh noticed Spence grinning at the antics of two small frogs.

"You like it here in Hope, don't you, Spence?" she asked.

"I must. I seem to be spending a lot of time here. And my sisters haven't kicked me out yet."

"That's good," Ryleigh said with a chuckle.

"Agreed," Spence said, squeezing Ryleigh's hand. "I'm glad Emma and Bailey moved here to Hope. I never would have met you otherwise."

"I was just thinking about that the other day," Ryleigh said, nodding. "My life has changed so much since I got out of school. I'm more relaxed, and a lot happier now. You're a big part of that, Spence."

"Glad I could help," Spence said, winking. "I hope you know that, although I love my sisters, they aren't why I've been spending so much time in Hope."

"They aren't?" Ryleigh asked quietly.

"No, Ryleigh, they aren't," Spence said. "Do you have any idea how incredible you are? You have such a good heart, Ryleigh. I see the way you interact with the kids. They really adore you. And I swear you're an animal whisperer. I've watched you instantly calm down the most frightened animals. Your rescue operation is the perfect fit for you. I'm glad you're letting me be a small part of it."

"You may not realize it, Spence, but you're a natural with animals," Ryleigh said.

Spence pulled Ryleigh into his arms and looked into her deep brown eyes. "I guess we're a good team then, aren't we?"

"I guess so," Ryleigh whispered, just before their lips met in a sweet kiss.

* * *

The concert was winding down and the bands were beginning to pack up their gear. As Spence and Ryleigh slowly worked their way back across the park to rejoin the family, they ran into Wyatt just leaving the elephant ear booth. He had a piping hot pastry in his hand, and a huge grin on his face.

Spence laughed and said, "Bro, you look like someone just gave you the last cookie in the cookie jar!"

"Close," Wyatt replied as he stuffed a piece of pastry into his mouth. "This was the last elephant ear before they shut down. Hot out of the fryer!"

Ryleigh laughed as Spence ripped off a piece of the elephant ear and stuffed it in his mouth.

Wyatt tore off a large piece of the pastry and handed it to Ryleigh. Turning to his brother, he asked, "Are you going home with Dad and Mom in the morning, Spence?"

"No. I brought my laptop with me. I think I'll spend the week at Emma and Matt's."

"I brought mine too," Wyatt said. "Maybe I'll ask Bailey if she and Aiden care if I stick around for a week. Since the concert is over, maybe we could find something else to do tomorrow."

"Hey," Ryleigh said, "you know what would be fun? We should take Wyatt up to Paradise Lake. He'd love it!"

"That's a good idea, Ryleigh," Spence agreed. "Maybe we could even borrow fishing poles from your family and do a little fishing. What do you say, Wyatt?"

"I'm game!" Wyatt said. "But, are you sure you want me tagging along to the lake?"

"It'll be fun!" Ryleigh said as she linked arms with the boys. "We could make a day of it. We could even take Sage and Jack along. They love going to the lake."

Arms still linked together, the trio walked up to the rest of the family and Spence announced, "Wyatt and I aren't going home tomorrow. We're going to stay here for a week."

As he gathered a couple of lawn chairs, Joe laughed and said, "Why am I not surprised? It's getting to the point where we have to come to Hope if we want to see our kids. We may as well move over here!"

Mike picked up Coco and tucked her under his arm. "Well, Joe, your sons-in-law *did* just finish building a couple of houses."

Chapter Eighteen

Armed with fishing gear and a cooler of cold drinks and food, Ryleigh, Spence, and Wyatt began loading the car for a trip to the lake. Jack and Sage stuck close to the car as it was being loaded. They both enjoyed going to the lake and did not want to be left behind. After Ryleigh reminded the dogs to be on their best behavior, Spence picked up Sage and put her in the front seat with him, and Jack jumped into the back seat with Wyatt.

The closer they got to the lake, the more excited the dogs became. By the time Ryleigh parked the car, the boys were laughing at the dogs' antics. Sage constantly turned in the front seat so she could see Jack, and they both wagged their tails furiously. It was all Spence and Wyatt could do to attach their leashes before letting them out of the car.

Spence grabbed the small cooler and a blanket from the trunk of the car while Wyatt gathered the fishing gear. Ryleigh took both dogs on their leashes, and they all headed down the trail toward the lake. Sage kept tugging at the end of her leash, wanting to explore, but Jack was content to walk along the trail, seemingly in no hurry.

When they broke through the trees and Wyatt saw the lake for the first time, he had the same reaction Spence had the first time he went to Paradise with Ryleigh.

"Wow!" Wyatt said as he walked toward the lake. "The water is crystal clear. Do the dogs ever go swimming here?"

Ryleigh smiled as she dropped the dogs' leashes and they walked to the edge of the lake, immediately lapping up some of the water.

"Sometimes," Ryleigh replied. "They love the water. It's fun watching them splash around in the lake with each other. They're like a couple of kids."

"Next time I come over," Wyatt said, "I'm bringing swimming trunks to leave at Bailey's in case we come up to the lake."

Wyatt dropped the fishing poles, tore off his shoes and socks, and waded into the lake.

"I thought we came up here to go fishing," Spence laughed. "Those fish will get one look at your big feet, and you'll scare them off!"

"Then I won't have to clean any fish," Wyatt retorted. "Sounds like a win to me."

Ryleigh chuckled at the brothers' good-natured sparring as she spread the blanket on the ground. Before long, she and Spence had cast their lines in the water and kicked back on the blanket waiting for the fish to bite. In the meantime, Wyatt continued playing in the water with the dogs.

Eventually, Wyatt and both dogs got tired of playing in the water and walked over to the blanket.

Wearing a mischievous grin, Wyatt looked at the wet dogs and said, "You can't get on the blanket while you're wet. You need to shake off first."

Right on cue, Jack and Sage shook furiously, spraying water all over Ryleigh and Spence. Then they triumphantly curled up on a corner of the blanket to nap.

"You'd better keep both eyes open, Wyatt," Spence laughed. "Ryleigh and I may drag you over and toss you in the lake!"

After relaxing for a couple of hours, watching the dogs, and not doing much fishing, Spence decided he was hungry. Everyone reeled in their fishing lines and settled in to have sandwiches and chips for lunch. Once they were finished eating, Ryleigh gathered up the remnants of lunch and packed things back into the cooler.

Since the fishing lines were already out of the water, they decided they were done fishing for the day and would just enjoy the beautiful weather. Jack curled up beside the blanket while Sage explored a few yards away.

Several minutes later, Spence heard an odd guttural sound. He looked over at Jack and asked, "What's with Jack?"

"That's a low growl," Wyatt said. "Look, the hair is standing up on the back of his neck."

Ryleigh looked around for Sage and saw her near a patch of bushes about twenty yards away.

"Sage," she called, "come here, girl."

Sage had just turned in Ryleigh's direction when there was a rustling in the bushes behind her. Suddenly, a coyote lunged from the bushes and grabbed Sage. In an instant, Jack rushed over and pounced on the coyote. He attacked the wild animal with all the fury of a prizefighter, shaking him furiously until the coyote dropped the small dog. Yipping and howling, Sage limped over to Ryleigh.

In the meantime, Spence grabbed a piece of firewood lying on the ground and approached the coyote.

"Spence!" Ryleigh screamed. "Don't throw it. You might hit Jack."

"That's a wild animal, Spence!" Wyatt yelled. "Be careful!"

The three young adults felt helpless as Jack battled the wild coyote. Growling, barking, and painful howls filled the air as the two animals became one mass of flying fur. Finally, Jack summoned all his strength, got a good hold on the coyote, and flung him off to the side. The bloodied coyote howled and ran off into the woods.

Exhausted, Jack fell to the ground, panting and suffering from several bloody wounds. Spence and Wyatt rushed over to Jack, while Ryleigh walked up slowly, still cradling Sage in her arms.

Spence looked up at Ryleigh. "This doesn't look good, Ryleigh. He's bleeding pretty badly."

"Oh, God, no," Ryleigh whispered.

Wyatt grabbed the blanket from the ground and brought it over to Jack. He knelt beside the injured dog and carefully wrapped him in the blanket.

"Spence, take Sage from Ryleigh," Wyatt instructed. "Ryleigh, grab the fishing gear. I'll take Jack in the back seat with me. Spence will take Sage. You need to drive, Ryleigh. You know the road better than we do."

Everyone rushed into action, running back down the trail toward the car. Within minutes, Ryleigh sped out of the parking lot and headed down the mountain to town. She immediately put her cell phone on speaker and called Kevin Draper to tell him what happened and alert him that they were on their way. She then called her dad and asked him to meet them at the veterinary clinic.

Ryleigh quickly glanced over at Sage, shuddering in Spence's lap and bleeding from a few small wounds. Tears began rolling down her cheeks as she tried to focus on the road.

Spence put his hand on Ryleigh's arm. "It'll be okay, Ryleigh," he said quietly, not even sure he believed that himself.

* * *

When Ryleigh screeched to a stop in front of Draper's clinic, several people were on the sidewalk waiting for them. Larry Draper immediately took Jack from Wyatt's arms in the back seat, while Kevin took Sage from Spence. Not bothering with the waiting gurney, Larry ran into the clinic with the severely injured dog.

As he rushed past his son, Larry said, "I'm taking Jack right into surgery. Kevin, you take care of Sage."

Once both dogs were being taken care of, Travis pulled his daughter into a tight hug. No words were necessary at the moment. When everyone caught their breath, Travis led his daughter into the clinic, followed by Spence and Wyatt. And they waited.

Time seemed to stand still. Kevin finally emerged from one of the exam rooms and pulled up a chair in front of Ryleigh.

"Sage is resting," he said. "I gave her a light sedative so I could stitch up her wounds. None of them are too bad, but some did require stitches. I also x-rayed her front leg. It has a small hairline fracture, so I put a cast on it to protect it. You can go back and see her in a few minutes."

"What about Jack?" Ryleigh asked as tears cascaded down her cheeks once again.

"He's still in surgery. We'll know more when Dad finishes."

Kevin put his hand on Ryleigh's and said, "Dad's the best veterinarian around, Ryleigh. Jack is in good hands. If anyone can bring him through this, it's my dad. With God's guidance."

Kevin then led them back to see Sage, a much-needed distraction while they awaited news about Jack.

Sage was still a bit groggy, and had stitches in a couple of places on her head and neck, but she weakly wagged her tail when they entered the room.

Ryleigh looked at Kevin and asked, "Can I pick her up?"

"Sure," Kevin answered with a smile. "She would probably like that. You can take her home when you go. I'll go check on surgery. You guys can take Sage back to the waiting room with you, and I'll let you know what I find out."

Nearly an hour later, both the Drapers joined the others in the waiting room. Larry pulled up a chair and sank into it.

"Ryleigh, I know you want the truth," Larry began. "This is going to be a tough one. Jack lost a lot of blood. I treated all his wounds. Some of them were pretty deep. He's resting comfortably now, but he's heavily sedated. It could be touch and go for a while. But I think if he makes it through the night, he'll probably be fine. He just won't be fighting any more coyotes."

"I know he's still sedated, Dr. Draper," Ryleigh said, "but can we go see him?"

Larry looked around the group before answering. "Okay, sure. He doesn't look pretty, so be sure you're ready."

When Ryleigh walked into Jack's room with Sage in her arms, the worried dog began whimpering and trying to wiggle out of her arms. Ryleigh looked at the senior vet and he simply nodded.

Ryleigh held Sage down close to Jack and she gently licked his face as tears formed in the little dog's eyes. Ryleigh then laid Sage beside Jack and she instantly snuggled in close, resting her head on Jack's front leg.

"Sage and I are staying here tonight," Ryleigh announced.

Larry looked at Travis, who shrugged.

"You don't need to stay, Ryleigh," he said. "The night vet tech will be here, and she'll keep an eye on Jack. Why don't you take Sage home and let her rest?"

Ryleigh started to pick up Sage and was met with bared teeth and a weak growl.

Spence chuckled, and said, "It looks like Sage doesn't plan to go anywhere."

Larry Draper was a wise man who knew how to pick his battles.

He patted Sage on the head and said, "Okay, little lady, you win. I guess it's only fair. You rescued Jack, then he rescued you. That means you've earned the right to stay with him."

"If Sage gets to stay, I'm staying," Ryleigh said adamantly.

"Okay," Larry said with a smile. "I know when I've been beat. Make yourself as comfortable as you can, and I'll be back early in the morning. Help yourself to anything you want in the kitchen. You probably still remember your way around."

"Thanks, Dr. Draper," Ryleigh said.

Spence put his arm around Ryleigh's waist and pulled her close. "Are you going to be okay?"

"Yeah," she replied, looking at the two boys. "Besides, you guys need to get out of those bloody clothes. I'll see you in the morning."

"Okay," Spence replied before pulling her into a kiss.

After saying their goodbyes, Travis and the boys left the building.

As they walked down the sidewalk together, Spence said, "Travis, I plan to marry your daughter, so I hope you're okay with that."

Travis smiled at Spence without missing a step and said, "I know you do, son. And, yes, I'm okay with it."

Chapter Nineteen

Early the next morning, Travis pulled into the parking lot at Draper's clinic and chuckled to see Mike Slater standing at the door waiting for the clinic to open. He had called Mike late last night to let him know what happened. Mike was going to rush over to the clinic, but Travis convinced him it wasn't necessary, and told him Ryleigh was spending the night with Jack and Sage.

Travis walked up and shook hands with Mike just as the vet assistant unlocked the front door.

"When you said you would stop by sometime today," Travis said with a chuckle, "I didn't think that meant you would be standing here waiting for them to unlock the front door."

As the two men entered the clinic, Mike asked, "Have you heard how Jack's doing?"

"No," Travis said. "When I talked to Ryleigh last night, she said he was still heavily sedated. I'm sure we'll find out something in a few minutes."

"Pastor Harmon," the assistant began, "you guys can go on back to Jack's room if you want to. Doctor Draper should be here in a few minutes. He plans to check on Jack as soon as he gets here."

"Thanks, Michelle," Travis said as he and Mike headed to the back of the clinic.

When they entered Jack's room, Ryleigh was slumped over in a chair she had pulled close to Jack's bed. Sage was still curled up beside Jack, with her head tucked close to his head. Mike walked over quietly and petted the top of Sage's head before putting his hand on Jack's back.

Travis placed his hand on Ryleigh's shoulder. When she looked up at her dad, he could tell she hadn't slept much during the night.

"Ryleigh, go home and get some sleep."

"Later, Dad," she replied.

"Spence said he's going to be up to relieve you in about an hour," Travis continued.

"He did?" Ryleigh asked.

"Yes, he did," Travis smiled. "When he gets here, I want you to go home and get some rest."

A few minutes later, Larry Draper walked into the room. He took one look at Ryleigh and shook his head with a smile. "I'm not surprised to see you're still here. You never could walk away from an animal."

Patting Sage on the head, Larry pulled out his stethoscope to listen to Jack's heart. After checking him over, he gently stroked the dog's head before replacing his IV bottle.

Larry tucked his stethoscope into the pocket of his lab coat, and said, "Well, he made it through the night, so that's the first big hurdle. His heart sounds strong and his vital signs are all good. I'm going to start weaning him off the sedative today to see how he does."

Looking at Ryleigh, he chuckled, "I'm not sure Sage will let me move her. Why don't you see if you can take her outside before you leave, then I'll have Michelle give her a little breakfast. After breakfast, she can come back in to be with Jack. I think it's good for both of them that she insisted on staying."

After Ryleigh left to take Sage outside, Mike turned to Larry. "I've known you for a long time, Larry, so I know this goes without saying. But, please do everything you can for Jack. I don't care what it costs. Just do what you can."

Larry patted Mike on the back and shook Travis's hand. "You know I will, Mike. I'll take care of Jack, and you guys take care of Ryleigh. I swear, that girl should have been a veterinarian!"

* * *

Ryleigh and Spence spent the next four days on a round-the-clock vigil with Jack. Spence stayed at the clinic with Ryleigh and the dogs throughout the day, and Ryleigh continued staying overnight. Eventually, Spence refused to take no for an answer and sent Ryleigh home to shower and sleep in her own bed. Sage only left Jack's side long enough to go outside. She would eat only if they sat the food bowl beside Jack. She spent all her time curling up next to Jack, usually resting her head on his front leg.

A steady stream of friends and family stopped by to check on Jack and marvel over the heroic dog. By the end of the third day, Jack had been weaned off the sedative and began eating a small amount of soft food. Larry Draper wanted to keep him at the clinic for one more day as a precaution.

When Jack was released from the clinic, there was quite a gathering of people on the sidewalk waiting to greet him. Most of Ryleigh's family was there, including the kids who had not been able to see Jack or Sage since the incident. Joe and Hannah Campbell had come over from Seattle, and several people from Hope came out to see Jack after hearing how he fought off a coyote.

Before leaving the clinic, Spence attached Jack's leash and was slowly working their way toward the front door. Ryleigh had Sage on her leash, right beside Jack. When Mike opened the door, both dogs limped out to greet the crowd. Sage still had a cast on her front leg, and Jack looked like he had gone to battle, but both dogs wagged their tails.

Aaron and Sophie rushed over and knelt beside the two injured dogs, softly talking to them.

"Be gentle with them, kids," Kaci reminded. "They have both been hurt badly. They're going to need lots of rest."

Two-year-old Levi slowly approached Jack, glancing back at his dad for reassurance, and gently put his arm around the dog's neck. With tears in his eyes, Levi leaned over and kissed Jack's head.

"I love you, Jack," the little boy said. "Get better, 'kay?"

Levi then walked over to Sage and looked at the cast on her leg. Pointing to the cast, he asked, "What's that?"

Ryleigh knelt beside her little nephew, put her arm around his waist, and pulled him close.

"That's a cast, Levi," she explained. "Sage broke her leg, so the cast will protect it while it heals."

"Oh," Levi said as he lightly touched the cast.

Travis picked up his young grandson and said, "We better get Jack and Sage home so they can rest."

"Can we ride with the dogs, Papa?" Aaron asked.

Travis looked to Ryleigh for her thoughts.

"Please, Papa?" Sophie pleaded. "We'll be careful."

"I'll tell you what," Ryleigh said, "let Spence lift Jack into the back seat, then you two can sit back there with him."

"What about Sage, Aunt Ryleigh?" Sophie asked.

"We're going to let Sage sit up front in Aunt Ryleigh's lap," Spence said.

"But who will drive?" Sophie asked in confusion.

Spence smiled and said, "I'll drive Aunt Ryleigh's car so she can take care of Sage."

Once the dogs were settled in Ryleigh's car, Larry Draper reached in the passenger window and placed his hand on Ryleigh's shoulder.

"You be sure to call us if you need anything, okay?"

"I will, Dr. Draper," Ryleigh said. "Thank you so much for everything. I don't know what we'd have done without you and Kevin. You two are lifesavers."

"One of us will stop by the house sometime tomorrow to check on them," Larry said.

"Thanks again, Larry," Travis said, shaking the senior vet's hand.

Looking into the back seat to be sure everyone was ready to go, Spence slowly pulled the car out of the parking lot and headed down the street, followed by several other vehicles.

* * *

Jack and Sage continued recuperating at home, where Jack was making good progress and getting stronger every day. The kids stopped by frequently to see the dogs and giggled when Sage ran up to them on three legs, wagging her tail in excitement. Even though they were anxious to run and play with the two dogs, they were satisfied to sit with them in the shade. Whenever the dogs decided to walk around a bit, they were followed by three kids who cautioned them to take it easy.

Between work and caring for Jack and Sage, Ryleigh welcomed her family's offer to handle things at the rescue operation. Spence had not gone home to Seattle since the dogs were injured. He worked from Emma and Matt's house and assured Ryleigh that things would be taken care of with the other animals. After working closely with Ryleigh since the operation opened, Spence slid seamlessly into her role, allowing her to focus on her two dogs. He even went with Travis to pick up another dog from the local humane shelter.

As Travis and Spence were getting the new dog settled into a spot in the rescue building, they heard a vehicle stop outside. A few minutes later, Mike walked in carrying a large bouquet of flowers and a small sack.

Travis chuckled at his friend and said, "Mike, you shouldn't have! I'm not much of a flower person. I would have preferred chocolate."

Mike laughed, and said, "Then it's a good thing they aren't for you."

Spence smiled as he took the flowers and bag from Mike. "These are for me. Well, not exactly for me. Mike graciously agreed to run an errand for me this afternoon while we were busy with the new dog."

Turning to Mike, he said, "Thanks for picking these up, Mike. You didn't have any problem, did you? Everything was already paid for."

"No problem at all," Mike said. "Things were ready when I got there."

"So," Travis began, "are you guys going to tell me what's going on? Or do you plan to keep me in suspense?"

"I can't keep you in suspense, Travis," Spence said, smiling. "Because I'm going to need your help in a few minutes. Mike stopped by the florist to pick up the flowers I ordered yesterday."

Grinning, Spence held up the small bag and said, "Then he stopped by the jewelry store to pick up this ring."

Smiling, Travis said, "Boy, Spence, when you decide to do something, you don't waste any time."

"No, I don't," Spence laughed. "Ryleigh knows we were picking up a new dog. What I'd like you to do is tell her I need to get her opinion on something about the dog. That way she'll come down here so I can ask her to marry me."

Mike patted Travis on the shoulder and said, "And I don't think our presence is required, so why don't I run you back to the house and you can send Ryleigh up here."

As the two men started for the door, Spence asked nervously, "Travis, Ryleigh *will* say yes, won't she?"

Travis patted Spence on the back and said confidently, "I have no doubt she will say yes."

Fifteen minutes later, Spence heard the quad pull up out front and Ryleigh walked in the door.

Not seeing Spence in the common area, Ryleigh called out for him.

"I'm back here in the last room."

Assuming that's where he put the new dog, Ryleigh walked in and looked around in surprise, not seeing an animal.

Spence got up from a chair in the corner and knelt on one knee in the middle of the room, holding flowers in one hand and a ring box in the other.

Covering her mouth with her hands, Ryleigh gasped as tears filled her eyes.

"Ryleigh," Spence began, "by now you've got to know how much you mean to me. When we first met before Bailey and Emma's wedding, I knew you were special. As much as I hoped you would fall in love with Seattle when you moved there, I knew your heart belonged here in Hope. You have the biggest heart of anyone I know, so I hope you have room in that heart for me. I love you, Ryleigh, and I can't imagine my life without you. Will you marry me?"

"Yes, Spence," Ryleigh replied as tears ran down her cheeks. "Yes, I'll marry you. I love you too."

As she wiped her tears with one hand, she looked around the room smiling, and said, "I just have one question."

"What's that?"

"Where's the new dog?"

They laughed as Spence stood, pulled his future wife into his arms, and kissed her tenderly. He then slid the perfectly-sized ring onto her finger.

"Shall we go tell everyone the good news?" Spence asked.

"Absolutely!" Ryleigh replied excitedly. Looking around the room again, she added, "But seriously, where's the dog? Is there *really* another dog? Or did you and Dad just make that up?"

Spence took Ryleigh's hand and led her to another cubicle. "Rex is right here, safe and sound at Ryleigh's Rescue. And he's quite real. Not made up at all. Now, future Mrs. Campbell, why don't you let me give you a ride on the quad, and we'll go tell the family the news."

As Ryleigh climbed on the quad behind Spence, holding her flowers in one hand, she laughed and said, "Sage and Jack are going to be so excited. I hope you realize they will both be at the wedding."

Spence laughed as he started the quad and said, "I don't doubt that at all! Hopefully, you can keep the wedding party to just the two dogs!"

"I make no promises, Mr. Campbell!"

Chapter Twenty

While Ryleigh's life remained busy with work and running the rescue operation, the construction of her house continued. By the time Jack and Sage had fully recovered from the coyote attack, the house was nearly complete. Ryleigh had been feeling neglectful in her friendship with Amy, so she invited her over to walk through the house to check for any last-minute touchups that might be needed.

Ryleigh was walking around the outside of her house with her mom when Amy pulled into the recently paved driveway. Being eight months pregnant, Amy slowly climbed out of the car and met Ryleigh and Meghan in the driveway.

"How are you feeling, Amy?" Meghan asked.

Amy chuckled and said honestly, "I'm ready for this pregnancy to be over."

"I'm sure," Meghan said, placing her hand on Amy's back. "That last month can be a little difficult."

"It's been brutal!" Amy said, laughing, as she reached out to hug her best friend.

"I'm sorry I haven't been a very good friend lately," Ryleigh apologized. "Since I moved back home, I was hoping to be more involved during your pregnancy. You know, helping you out more when you needed something. Maybe rescuing you from my brother so we could have some lunches together."

"You've been a little busy, Ryleigh," Amy laughed. "I don't know what it is about your family. None of you can limit yourselves to one project at a time. You've been busy with work, building a new house, setting up an animal rescue operation, and falling off mountains. Not to mention getting engaged!"

"Yeah, I guess life has been a bit intense," Ryleigh said smiling. "But I think it's going to slow down now. I really do."

"Let's see," Amy said as she began counting on her fingers. "You're still working. You're still rescuing animals. You will now be getting ready to move into your new home. And you have a wedding to plan. Sure, that sounds like life is going to slow down."

Meghan chuckled as she shook her head. "That *is* slowing down for Ryleigh! I'm going to head back home and let you girls check out the inside of the house. Have fun!"

Amy stopped to look at the house as she and Ryleigh walked up the sidewalk. "I love the design of your house, Ryleigh. Your mom is such a talented designer."

"She's great. It always amazed me that she designed the house I grew up in. And every home she's designed for the family has a unique feel. They certainly aren't cookie-cutter houses."

Ryleigh linked arms with Amy as they stepped onto the front porch. "We need to do lunch this week. No excuses. Unless, of course, you decide to have that baby early."

Once inside, the two young women strolled through the house, admiring the new home and checking for any flaws that would need attention. Almost an hour later, they returned to the living room.

"I'm no expert, Ryleigh," Amy began, "but I didn't notice a single thing that needed to be fixed."

"I didn't either. The guys do great work. Dad and Uncle Todd are sticklers for details. I would honestly be surprised if I did find anything wrong. But I know Aiden and Matt want to give it a final look before pronouncing it finished."

"By the way," Amy began, "I love the colors you picked. Did Spence help you pick them out?"

Ryleigh laughed. "No. He said he would be happy with whatever colors I chose. He's honestly having a hard time thinking of it as *our* house. I have to keep reminding him."

"Your brother was no help deciding on colors for our house either," Amy chuckled. "And we were already married! Maybe it's a guy thing. Don't worry about Spence. He'll be fine. There's just been a lot going on!"

"You can say that again!"

Once they were back outside, Amy looked around and asked, "When are you having the sod put in?"

"They're going to start the underground sprinklers tomorrow. As soon as that's finished, the sod will go in. Then it will truly look like a finished home."

"That means you should be able to move in before the end of the month, right?"

"I think so," Ryleigh said. "Once I get moved in, then I can concentrate on planning the wedding."

"Have you and Spence set a date yet?"

"Not yet. But neither of us wants a long, drawn-out engagement. So, my guess would be within six months."

Amy linked arms with Ryleigh as they walked toward the car. "That's so exciting! If you need any help planning the wedding, let me know."

"Definitely! Hey, are you in a hurry to get back home?"

"Not particularly," Amy replied. "Levi is hanging out at the center with Josh today. He's been pretty good about taking Levi down there a couple of days a week to give me a break."

"Let's go have lunch today! My treat! Do you feel like Luigi's or the deli?"

"Ah, some girl time," Amy sighed. "How about the deli? I could eat a nice nutritious sandwich and a salad, then follow it up with one of their yummy brownies."

Ryleigh laughed. "I knew you were my best friend for a reason!"

* * *

Travis and Todd put together a rather impressive work party when it came time to lay sod at Ryleigh's house. Joe and Hannah brought Wyatt over and, of course, Spence was still in town. Aiden and Matt were sending over a couple of the guys from one of their crews, and JC had several teenagers from the center who offered to help. It would take a couple of long days to sod the large yard, but then the house would be officially finished.

Since Spence's family would be in town to help with the sod project, he and Ryleigh decided that would be a good time to discuss wedding plans and show everyone the finished house. Although Spence had helped out on the house quite a bit during construction, he hadn't been inside since before it was painted.

Spence and Ryleigh strolled hand in hand up the road to the new house. When they reached the driveway, they stopped and looked at the large yard, all graded and prepped for sod.

Ryleigh turned to Spence and handed him the key to the front door.

"I've seen the finished house already," she said. "You haven't. Let's go look at our new home."

"It's a beautiful home, Ryleigh," Spence said as he put his arm around her waist. "I'm glad your dad and Todd allowed me to help with some of the work. I sure learned a lot from them!"

"And someday you'll be able to tell our kids that you helped build our house."

"And Grandma designed it!" Spence said. "That still amazes me."

"Our house was truly a family affair. Your dad and mom, all three of your siblings… I think everyone in both our families helped in some way."

"That's what it's all about, Ryleigh. I love how supportive your entire family is. I am so blessed to be joining your family."

"I feel the same way about your family," Ryleigh said, smiling. "They were like my second family while I lived in Seattle. I don't think I could have survived my time over there without you and Wyatt."

"Shall we go check out the house?" Spence asked, dangling the key in front of Ryleigh.

"Absolutely! You're going to love the colors I picked for the interior."

"As long as you didn't paint the walls hot pink, I'm sure I will love anything you chose."

"Oh," Ryleigh said, feigning concern, "you don't like hot pink? We might have a problem."

As Spence put the key into the lock, he chuckled and said, "I think I'm safe. You're not a hot pink kind of girl."

The young couple spent an hour wandering through the house, looking in all the cabinets, and admiring the view from the windows. They then went through the dining room, out the French doors, and sat down on the steps to the back deck.

"We're going to need to get some chairs for the deck," Spence said, grinning.

"We need furniture for inside the house too!" Ryleigh pointed out. "I don't know about you, but I certainly don't have much to furnish a house."

"I don't either. Especially since Wyatt and I share an apartment. But we can get a little at a time. It's not a big deal."

"You know, Spence," Ryleigh began, "since you've been staying with Matt and Emma, there's no reason you can't move some of your stuff over from Seattle whenever you want to. I'll be moving into the house sometime after the sod is finished. *You* obviously can't move in until after the wedding, but there's no reason you can't move some of your non-essentials into the house before then."

"I suppose that's true. I'll think about that once we settle on a date for the wedding and make some of those plans."

"Hopefully, the sod will go quickly with all the help we'll have," Ryleigh said. "That way we should have some time to get together with the family and discuss the wedding."

"I plan to be thinking about a wedding date while I'm laying sod," Spence said.

"I guarantee Dad will fire you from the crew if he finds you writing out a date with the sod," Ryleigh laughed.

"I don't know," Spence chuckled, "I bet Todd would think it's hilarious!"

* * *

Thanks to the many people working to lay sod, the project finished sooner than expected and the lawn looked great. The family now had the entire afternoon and evening, if necessary, to relax and discuss wedding plans. After everyone had a chance to tour the house, the whole family gathered at Aiden and Bailey's house next door. Mike had made special arrangements for Luigi's to deliver pizza, large pans of lasagna, and all the trimmings for dinner. In the meantime, everyone could relax.

"Ryleigh, I just love your home!" Hannah said. "It was so much fun to help with some of the little jobs during construction. And, Travis, you were such a patient teacher. Thanks for showing me how to do some of those things. Who would have thought I would have been helping run electrical wires?"

"Spence and I were just talking about that yesterday," Ryleigh said, smiling. "The house was definitely a family project. Everyone got involved. And we sure appreciate everyone's help!"

"Well, does anyone want to help us plan a wedding?" Spence asked, looking around the room.

"I do!" Amy said, enthusiastically.

"Bailey and I want to help plan our brother's wedding too!" Emma said. She laughed and added, "I still can't believe you convinced Ryleigh to marry you, Spence."

Spence shook his head and said sarcastically, "Aren't little sisters great?"

JC laughed and said, "Well, they do give you someone to pick on."

With Coco curled up on his lap, Mike chuckled and spoke up from his spot at the end of the sofa. "Before the discussion gets completely derailed, I'd like to say something. Ryleigh and Spence, I want you to know I have an account set up at the furniture store for you. Whenever you're ready, go get what you need."

Ryleigh and Spence looked at each other, then back at Mike.

"You don't need to do that, Mike," Spence said.

Mike laughed and said, "I guess you haven't been around long enough to know I rarely do what I need to. I don't want any arguments. I did the same thing for the other kids, so I want to do this for you, too. End of discussion."

"Wow," Spence said as he and Ryleigh jumped up to thank Mike.

"That's very generous of you, Mike," Joe said.

Mike simply waved his hand. "It's no big deal. Let's discuss wedding plans."

Spence took Ryleigh's hand as she sat beside him on the loveseat.

"Well, we haven't decided on an actual date yet," Spence began. "But last night we decided we want to get married in the middle of October. We both like the early fall season. And we've made a few other decisions, then we'll get ideas from the rest of you about whatever else we need to do.

"Bailey, since you're now the Senior Pastor at Hope Community Church, and you just happen to be my sister, we'd like you to officiate the ceremony."

"I'd love to," Bailey said. "You'll be my first wedding!"

"You'll do great, Bailey," Ryleigh added, looking at her dad. "You had the best mentor around."

"I understand it's a family tradition to have Aaron as the ring bearer and Sophie as the flower girl," Spence said, grinning. "Are you two okay with that?"

"Yes!" the kids said simultaneously.

"Wyatt," Spence said, "I can't imagine having anyone other than my twin brother as my best man. I assume that works for you?"

"You can count on me, little brother," Wyatt said, nodding.

Ryleigh looked over at Amy and said, "Amy, you're my best friend. I was thrilled when you asked me to be your maid of honor. I would love for you to be my matron of honor."

"Thanks, Ryleigh," Amy said. "I'd love to."

"Dad," Ryleigh said, "obviously I want you to walk me down the aisle."

"It'll be my pleasure, Ryleigh," Travis agreed, his eyes glistening.

Spence looked at his future wife and grinned. "Do you want to tell them the other thing you decided, or do you want it to be a surprise?"

"We're going to have two additional attendants," Ryleigh said, grinning. "Sage and Jack are going to be part of the wedding party."

"That's awesome!" Aaron yelled excitedly.

Smiling, Meghan looked at her youngest daughter and shook her head. "That doesn't surprise me at all."

Travis nudged Joe with his elbow. "The real surprise will be if she *only* has the two dogs at the wedding!"

Chapter Twenty-One

Work didn't slow down just because Ryleigh's life was busy. She finished a major project well before the deadline and was scheduled to attend a presentation meeting at the office in Seattle. Since she had to go to Seattle anyway, Spence decided to ride along and bring back some of his things from the apartment.

They got an early start over the pass since Ryleigh's meeting was at ten o'clock. After making a quick stop along the road for breakfast, they switched drivers so Spence could drop Ryleigh off at the office.

"Are you nervous about your presentation, Ryleigh?" Spence asked when they pulled back out onto the freeway.

"Not really," she replied. "I probably should be nervous since it's one of our largest clients. But Sam will be there, and she always has a calming effect on people. She said it's a great presentation. So, if she's not nervous about it, I probably don't need to be either."

"You'll do great," Spence said confidently.

"You know, Ryleigh, I was thinking about something the other day. At some point, I probably need to buy my own car. Wyatt and I have shared a car the entire time we've lived in Seattle. Since we shared an apartment, and parking can be a pain, it didn't make sense to have two cars. Now that I'll be moving to Hope permanently, I should give Wyatt our car and get my own."

"That's not a bad idea," Ryleigh agreed. "There's no big hurry, though. You can use my car whenever you need to."

"Have you decided when you're going to move into the house?" Spence asked, glancing at Ryleigh.

"I've been so busy finishing this project that I haven't done much packing yet. I'll have a little break after the presentation, though. I don't have a lot to pack, so hopefully I can get moved this weekend. Maybe we can go look at furniture sometime this week if you have time."

Spence shook his head and said, "I still can't believe Mike is paying for our furniture. That guy is unbelievable."

"He sure is. He's been completely financing the rescue operation and insisted on paying all the vet bills for Jack and Sage. But I remember he did the same thing for JC and Amy when they got married. And for Aiden and Bailey, and Matt and Emma. So, I shouldn't have been surprised. It seems like his generosity never ends."

"I haven't known him for very long," Spence said, "but he's amazing. He doesn't have any family in the area?"

"No," Ryleigh said. "He doesn't have any family left. I remember Dad saying he had one brother who passed away several years ago. Mike's wife died not long after they got married, and he never remarried. So, he's kind of adopted our family, and he fits in like he's always been part of the family."

Spence was quiet for several minutes, then a grin slowly spread across his face.

Ryleigh looked at him and smiled. "What? What are you thinking about that put a smile on your face?"

"Oh, nothing really."

Ryleigh laughed and said, "Come on. No secrets, remember?"

"I was just thinking," Spence said. "If Grandma makes it down for the wedding, we need to introduce her to Mike!"

"I've never met your Grandma. What's she like?"

"She's awesome! Grandma isn't someone you can describe. Grandma Campbell has to be experienced in person!"

* * *

After returning from Seattle, Spence insisted on storing his things in the garage at the new house. He told Ryleigh he didn't want to move any of his stuff into the house until after she had a chance to move in. Since she wasn't packed yet anyway, they decided to go furniture shopping, hoping some of the main pieces could be delivered before the weekend.

They spent the better part of the morning browsing at the furniture store and were able to decide on several items for their home. Spence insisted they not take advantage of Mike's generosity. So, they had agreed to get only the main things they would need. Luckily, the store manager said everything they purchased was in stock and could be delivered in a few days.

By the time moving day arrived, the furniture had been delivered. Travis and Meghan helped Ryleigh load her belongings into his pickup, and the trio headed to the house.

JC, Amy, and Levi were waiting for them when they pulled into the driveway.

Ryleigh walked over, hugged Amy, and picked up her nephew. "I didn't expect to see you guys here this morning."

"We have a doctor's appointment later," Amy said, smiling, "so I wanted to be here when you moved in."

"I'm glad you came over," Ryleigh said. Pointing a finger at Amy, she added, "But you are not to lift a single thing!"

Amy laughed. "Don't worry, I won't. I'm only here for moral support."

"And because Levi insisted he needed to help Aunt Ryleigh move," JC added, laughing.

Ryleigh squeezed Levi's little hand and said, "Thank you for helping, Levi. I'm sure I have something you can carry into the house for me."

"Yay!" Levi yelled as he squirmed out of her arms and headed straight for Papa.

"You're due next week, aren't you, Amy?" Meghan asked.

"Yes," Amy replied. "And we are both very ready!"

JC put his arm around his wife and said, "This is our last doctor's appointment before the delivery."

Amy looked around and asked, "Where's Spence?"

"He's been so busy helping me lately that he was getting a little behind at work," Ryleigh explained. "So, I told him we could handle what little I had to move, and he could get some work done."

"I'm sure it hasn't been easy for either of you to juggle everything that's been going on!" Amy said.

Ryleigh shrugged, smiling. "You just do what you've got to do. Working remotely definitely helps."

Meghan started to grab something from the back of the pickup and JC took it from her hands.

"Mom," JC said, "as long as I'm standing here, you don't need to help Dad unload the truck. You can make sure my stubborn wife stays out of trouble, and I can help Dad."

"Okay," Meghan laughed as she linked arms with her daughter-in-law. "Come on, Amy. I know when we're not needed."

Ryleigh watched her mom and best friend walk toward the house just as she felt a tug on her shirt.

"Aunt Wyleigh," Levi said, "me help, 'member?"

"I didn't forget, Levi," Ryleigh said. "I have something for you to carry into the house for me."

She reached into the cab of the pickup and pulled out a stuffed teddy bear. Handing it to Levi, she said, "This is a very special bear. Your daddy gave it to me when I moved away to school. Can you find a perfect spot for it in the house?"

Levi squeezed the bear tight and said, "Soft bear." Then he ran after his mom and grandma. "Wait for me, Mommy!"

"I can't believe you still have that bear, Ry," JC said, looking at his sister.

"Of course, I still have it," Ryleigh said. "It's a very special bear, remember?"

It didn't take the guys long to unload the truck. They carried in the last of the boxes, then joined the others in the living room.

Not long after JC sat down, Amy reached over and squeezed his hand.

"Honey, would you be upset if we skipped today's doctor's appointment?" Amy asked.

"Why would we want to skip it?" JC asked.

"Because I'm pretty sure we'll be at the hospital having the baby!" Amy said as she scooted to the edge of her seat.

Everyone was instantly on their feet as JC helped his wife up from the sofa.

"Mom," JC said as he looked around for his son, "can you take Levi?"

"Don't worry, Josh," Meghan said as she hurried to pick up her grandson. "We'll bring Levi with us. You worry about Amy."

As JC helped Amy to the car, she squeezed Ryleigh's hand and said, "Sorry to break up the party, Ryleigh. I seem to have a thing about having babies on moving day!"

"Oh, that's right!" Ryleigh said, laughing. "Levi was born the day you and JC moved into *your* new house. I had forgotten about that!"

Helping his wife into the car, JC turned to his family and said, "Okay, no one else in this family gets to move! I'm tired of filling houses with boxes *and* new humans on the same day! We'll see you all at the hospital!"

Travis chuckled as Ryleigh locked her front door and they hurried to their vehicles. "Never a dull moment in this family!"

Meghan kissed her husband and said, "You wouldn't have it any other way."

"You're right, honey," Travis said. "God is good."

As she climbed into her car, Ryleigh yelled, "All the time!"

* * *

Travis was unbuckling Levi from his car seat when he heard someone yell his name from across the parking lot.

"Travis, wait up!" John Phoenix yelled as he and his wife hurried across the hospital lot.

Meghan took Levi from her husband as Ryleigh joined them, and they waited for Amy's parents.

Travis shook John's hand and said, "Well, it looks like we're about to be grandparents again."

"It sure looks like it," John said, smiling.

"Amy called us while they were heading to the hospital," Vicki added.

About that time, Levi stretched his arms out toward Vicki. "Grandma!"

Meghan handed Levi off to Vicki. She happily took her only grandson and kissed his little cheek.

"Well, Levi," Vicki said, "should we go inside and wait for your new brother or sister?"

"Brother!" Levi yelled.

Everyone laughed and Ryleigh said, "Maybe. But you might get a new sister. Like Sophie is Aaron's little sister."

"Sister!" Levi yelled again.

"We'll have to wait to see what God gives us," Meghan said, squeezing her grandson's hand.

"God!" Levi yelled once more, obviously on a roll.

The family was all smiles as they entered the hospital and found their way to the maternity waiting room.

Travis was talking to the nurse at the nurse's station when Matt ran into the waiting room, followed by Mike.

"Are we too late?" Matt asked.

"We got here as fast as we could," Mike said, chuckling. "I'm surprised he didn't fall off the roof when JC called."

Travis laughed and patted Matt on the back. "You're not too late, Matt. I just talked to the nurse, and Amy is in the delivery room now. You may as well join the rest of the family while we wait."

Matt walked over to his parents, hugged his mom, and shook his dad's hand.

"How did you guys beat me here?" Matt asked, laughing.

"We were already in the car, heading to the grocery store when Amy called," Vicki said.

"So, we just made a detour," John added. "*You* apparently had to climb down from a roof. Good to see you made it safely, son."

For the next half an hour, the hospital waiting room filled up with more of JC and Amy's family. Kaci and Jason arrived with

Aaron and Sophie, who were very excited about getting a new cousin. Before long, the entire family was visiting while anxiously awaiting news about the baby's arrival.

Suddenly, JC appeared in the entryway to the waiting room. Everyone jumped up, eager to hear how the birth went.

JC held up his hand and said, "No, she hasn't had the baby yet. But she sent me out here to get her mother. Come on, Vicki" JC said, reaching for her hand. "Your daughter wants you in the delivery room with her."

Overcome with emotion, Vicki covered her face with her hands, then took JC's outstretched hand.

Turning to the rest of the family, he said, "I'll be out to give you the news after the baby is born."

Aaron and Sophie kept Levi busy in a play area in the corner of the waiting room while the adults visited. After several minutes, the kids began whispering, and then Sophie got up and walked over to Meghan.

"Grandma," she said quietly. "We're hungry."

Meghan glanced at the clock on the wall and said, "I'll just bet you are! It's past lunchtime."

Travis stood and said, "Jason, Matt, will you two come with me to the cafeteria? We'll bring back some lunch for everyone."

Sophie hugged her grandpa and said, "Thanks, Papa."

A short time later, everyone was busy gathering the trash from their lunch and didn't notice JC enter the room. Suddenly, Levi jumped up and ran across the room.

"Daddy!" Levi shouted, running into JC's arms. "Where's Mommy?"

"Mommy's a little busy right now," JC laughed. "You can see her in a little while, I promise."

Picking up his son, JC turned to his family. "It's a girl!" he said, beaming. "Amy and the baby are doing great, and everyone is healthy!"

Levi looked into his dad's face and asked, "Brother?"

JC chuckled and said, "No, Levi. You have a little sister."

"Sister?" Levi asked. "Yay! Sister!"

Chapter Twenty-Two

Amy was exhausted, but her face showed only pure love as she looked down at her daughter, cuddled against her chest. The baby was less than an hour old and had already captured her parents' hearts. Her Grandma Vicki stood quietly off to the side, allowing JC and Amy to bond with their new daughter.

With one hand resting on his wife's shoulder, and the other gently touching his daughter's head, JC asked, "Are you up to seeing any visitors yet, honey?"

"Sure," Amy smiled. "Why don't you bring Levi in to meet his new sister? And Dad and your parents." Amy then laughed and added, "And you'd better bring Matt back too. I don't think he would ever forgive me if he didn't get to meet his only niece on the day she was born."

JC chuckled and said, "Okay, I'll be right back."

Less than ten minutes later, with his two-year-old son sitting quietly in his arms, JC led the small group into Amy's hospital room. As the others stood back, he walked over to the side of his wife's bed and held Levi down for a closer look at the tightly wrapped bundle.

"Levi, this is your little sister."

Levi pointed a chubby little finger at the baby and whispered, "Sister?"

"Yes, your sister."

Levi reached for Meghan, who took him in her arms. Pointing to the baby again, he said quietly, "Grandma. My sister."

"Mom," Amy said, looking across the room, "do you want to hold your granddaughter?"

"Oh, yes," Vicki said quietly, as JC handed the baby to his mother-in-law.

She pulled the blanket away from the baby's face and ran her finger over the tiny nose.

"You're beautiful, little one," Vicki said with tears in her eyes. "Do you have a name yet?"

Amy took JC's hand in hers and said, "Her name is Allison Victoria Harmon."

"Victoria?" Vicki asked as tears ran down her cheeks.

"Yes, Mom," Amy said, smiling. "Her middle name is for you."

After several minutes, Vicki passed the baby to her husband.

"John," she said, "meet your new granddaughter."

John rocked his granddaughter in his arms and shook his head in amazement over the tiny bundle. He eventually passed Allison over to Travis and Meghan. After the grandparents took turns holding their newest grandchild and marveling over God's tiny miracles, the little girl was handed over to Matt.

Holding her gently, Matt looked into her tiny blue eyes and said, "Hey, Allie, I'm your Uncle Matt. If you ever need anything, just let me know. I'm a pretty good uncle, and I'll make sure nothing bad ever happens to you."

With the now sleeping bundle back in her arms, Amy said, "I'm sure there's a crowd of people out there waiting for news. Why don't you guys tell everyone they can meet the baby when we get home? And, Mom, Josh and I would love to have you tell them her name."

With tears forming in her eyes again, Vicki nodded as John pulled his wife into his arms.

Holding his squirming grandson in his arms, John and Vicki led the small group into the waiting room.

Before anyone could say a word, Levi blurted out, "Sister!"

The waiting room erupted in laughter as John sat the little boy down and he immediately ran to his cousins.

"Amy and the baby are doing great," John proudly told the family. "They look forward to seeing everyone when they get home, but now she needs to rest."

"Have they decided on a name yet?" Ryleigh asked.

Vicki squeezed her husband's hand as she said, "Her name is Allison Victoria Harmon. And she's absolutely beautiful. God is so good."

"All the time," John said, smiling. "All the time."

* * *

A large gathering of family members waited at JC and Amy's house to welcome them home. Vicki, Ryleigh, Bailey, and Emma had decorated the main living area with balloons and banners announcing the arrival of little Allison. Kaci and Meghan prepared large trays of snacks for the family. Mike had gifted the young family with a new bassinet for the baby. It was set up off to the side of the room, with a large teddy bear on the floor beside it – a gift from Allison's ecstatic cousins.

"They're here!" Aaron announced loudly. "Mom, can we go help them bring things in?"

"Sure," Kaci said. "Just be sure you're helping and not getting in the way."

As Aaron and Sophie ran toward the door, Sophie asked her brother, "Do you think they will let us carry her in?"

"Probably not," Aaron replied. "But maybe we'll get to hold her later."

While JC helped his wife out of the car, Ryleigh unlatched the baby's car seat from its base.

"Do you want to take the baby, or help Amy?" Ryleigh asked her brother.

JC smiled and said, "Go ahead and get Allison. I already have Amy. Besides, you haven't met your newest niece yet."

"That's right," Ryleigh said. "I have to start spoiling her before the rest of the family gets to her."

As they walked up the driveway, JC laughed. "With a family the size of ours, that little girl will be spoiled rotten before her first birthday."

Since they had time with the baby at the hospital, the grandparents were content to sit on the sofa and visit while the rest of the family met Allison. All the aunts, uncles, and cousins took turns holding the little girl. Even Mike spent some time getting to know her.

Mike was holding the baby while he quietly talked to her. "You're a cute one, Miss Allison. The kids all call me Mr. Mike. You'll be seeing me around here a lot. You're a lucky little girl. God blessed you with a wonderful family. Families don't come much better than yours. You be sure to let me know if there's ever anything you need, okay? You have a lot of people who love you, and you're going to grow into a beautiful young lady."

Ryleigh rested her head on Spence's shoulder as the family watched Mike's interaction with the baby.

"Mike would be such a great grandpa," Spence whispered to Ryleigh. "It's too bad he doesn't have kids or grandkids."

Sitting on the other side of Spence, JC quietly said, "Look around the room, Spence. This is Mike's family. He has a houseful of kids and grandkids."

As Spence looked around the room at the family he would be marrying into, he nodded.

"God is certainly good," Spence said.

From across the room, Mike replied as he held a sleeping baby, "All the time, son. All the time."

* * *

Although Ryleigh had moved most of her things to her home before the excitement of the new baby, she had not yet started living there. Her computer was still set up in the den of her parents' home, so she was working from there. She had decided not to move into her home until the yard was fenced. When she moved, she wanted to be able to take Sage and Jack with her. The fact that Amy and JC's new baby was right next door to her parents gave her another reason not to move. She enjoyed bonding with her newborn niece, something she had missed out on with the other kids. She also loved the girl time with her best friend so they could visit and discuss wedding plans.

After putting the baby down for a nap, Amy joined Ryleigh in the living room.

She sank into the easy chair and said, "I had forgotten how exhausting newborns are. And, of course, Levi wants to 'help' with everything. I'm glad he likes hanging out at the center with Josh once in a while. Then I can rest while Allison sleeps, instead of chasing after a little tornado."

Ryleigh laughed and said, "From what Mom says, Levi is just like JC was when he was that age. I, of course, was a little angel. You could always hope Allison will take after her Aunt Ryleigh!"

Amy laughed. "I'll keep my fingers crossed. I'm not sure I'll ever have enough energy for *two* little JCs!"

"You need to remember to take care of *you*, Amy, or you'll never have any energy. Make sure you take people up on their offers to watch Levi. I know Dad and Mom love having him around."

"Mom has offered to take him too," Amy said, smiling. "She's really gotten into the grandma role. I think she realizes what she missed with me and Matt."

"Yeah, I'm sure that's hard for her," Ryleigh said. "But it's great seeing your dad and mom involved with your kids. It's amazing the effect kids can have on people."

"It sure is," Amy said, nodding. "I still can't believe how much Dad and Mom's lives have changed in the past few years. It's incredible. They're finally the parents Matt and I always wanted and needed when we were growing up."

"I'm really happy for you, Amy," Ryleigh said as she reached for her friend's hand.

The two friends visited for over an hour while the baby slept, and thoroughly enjoyed working on wedding plans. Spence had told Ryleigh he was staying out of the wedding planning details. He insisted he would be happy with whatever she and her friends decided. He only needed to know what to wear and that she would be at the church on time. Ryleigh had gotten input from all the women in her life, including Spence's mom and sisters. She and Amy went over all the suggestions and decided on the decorations for the church, the flowers, and the wedding colors. She wasn't going to insist that Spence wear a tuxedo, instead opting for a gray suit with a lavender vest and tie to match the bride's colors.

"It looks like most of the wedding details have been decided, Ryleigh," Amy said. "You may be able to kick back and relax until the wedding."

"And finish moving into my house," Ryleigh laughed.

"When do you plan to start living there? The fencing is finished now, isn't it?"

"Yeah," Ryleigh said. "They finished it yesterday. I just need to bite the bullet and get moved. I'm dreading packing up my home office. That's the last thing left. I think I'll ask Spence if he can help me with that. He loves anything that involves computers. I know how to use them, but I don't want to deal with all the cables, connections, and stuff. He lives for that!"

"You're planning to move Sage and Jack to your house, right?"

"I am. That's why I needed to wait until the yard was fenced."

Amy smiled and said, "That won't make Levi happy. He plays with that dog every time he goes next door to Papa and Grandma's house. Half the time, he talks them into letting him bring Jack home with him! He honestly thinks Jack is his dog."

Ryleigh nodded in understanding. "I know he does. Maybe I'll ask him to help me set up Jack's dog house in my back yard. And I'll tell him he can visit Jack and Sage whenever he wants. As long as he has your permission."

"He would love to help you set up the dog house," Amy said. Then she laughed and said, "Between Jack, Sage, and all the animals at your shelter, don't be surprised if that little boy sets up camp in your back yard!"

Ryleigh laughed. "If he does, I promise to take good care of your son."

* * *

Jack and Sage had been running happily up and down the gravel access road between the two houses while Spence and Ryleigh moved the last of her things. Spence agreed to get her computer set up and operational while she handled the two dogs. JC and Levi met Ryleigh in the back yard of their parents' home to gather the dogs and their things for the move up the road.

Ryleigh felt a now familiar tug on her shirt. She looked down at her youngest nephew who had tears in his eyes. She sat down on the grass and pulled Levi into her lap.

"Aunt Wyleigh," the little boy began, "is Jack moving now?"

She snuggled him close as she tried to explain. "Yes, Levi. Jack and Sage are moving up to my house now."

"Why?" Levi asked as he struggled to understand.

"Because that's where I'll be living. I can't split up Sage and Jack, honey. They've been through a lot together and they need each other."

"I need Jack too," Levi said, tears running down his cheeks.

"Oh, sweetie," Ryleigh said, "you'll still have Jack. Remember, he's just going to be right up the road. Why don't you ride in the car with me to take the dogs to the house? Then maybe you can help me find the perfect place to set up Jack's dog house. Would you like to help me with that?"

As the little boy wiped his tears with his arm, a small smile formed as he nodded.

JC helped load the two dogs and his son into Ryleigh's car, then put the dog house and their belongings in his car. Ryleigh walked up to her brother and spoke quietly so Levi wouldn't hear. JC smiled and nodded, then they headed up the road.

The two dogs bounced out of the car and started running circles around the big fenced yard. Levi watched them, laughing, then followed behind as they explored their new boundaries. Ryleigh and JC watched Levi chase the dogs around the yard, laughing whenever he fell on the grass.

"Levi sure loves those dogs," Ryleigh said. "I hope it doesn't take him long to get used to not having them right next door."

JC put his arm around his sister's shoulder. "Don't worry about Levi, sis. He'll be fine. Besides, before we know it, he'll be five years old and disappearing down the road to visit Jack and Sage at your house."

"Or…" Ryleigh began with a grin. "You could get him his very own dog from Ryleigh's Rescue."

"Don't go there, Ry!" JC said, chuckling. "I now have two kids under the age of three. I don't need a dog to trip over too!"

"We'll see," Ryleigh laughed, then called for her nephew. "Levi, do you want to help us set up Jack's dog house now?"

"Yay!" Levi said, as he ran toward the house. "Come on, Jack!"

JC and Ryleigh stood in the yard, looking toward the back deck. They both put their hands on their hips, pretending to have trouble deciding where to put the dog house. Levi walked up beside them, mimicked them by putting his little hands on his tiny hips, then walked toward the deck.

Pointing to a spot next to the steps leading up to the deck, Levi announced, "Jack wants his house here."

Jack and Sage immediately curled up and laid down next to the steps.

Ryleigh laughed and said, "It looks like you chose the perfect spot, Levi. Good job!"

It didn't take long to set up the dog house and find a place on the deck for the food and water dishes. Ryleigh and JC sat on the steps and were soon joined by Spence, who had finished setting up Ryleigh's workstation.

Looking at Levi, sitting between the two dogs on the grass, Ryleigh asked, "Hey, Levi, how would you like to have a campout at my house tonight?"

"With Jack and Sage?" Levi asked excitedly.

"Yes, with Jack and Sage," Ryleigh said, smiling.

"And we get to sleep outside?"

"Absolutely!"

"Yay!" Levi yelled, hugging the two dogs. "Daddy, can I have my tent?"

Laughing, JC said, "Yes, son, I'll bring over your tent." Looking at his sister, JC added, "See what you started? You may never get rid of him now."

"Don't worry, JC. As I told your wife earlier, I promise to take good care of your son."

Chapter Twenty-Three

True to form, Ryleigh's life showed no signs of slowing down. She managed to get reasonably settled in her new home and still made occasional trips to Seattle for work projects. Spence had finally moved the last of his things from his apartment and had everything stored in the garage. Ryleigh's Rescue was frequently near capacity, but she followed her heart and never turned away an animal. After the pet adoption event, word spread quickly about the new shelter in town. Between Ryleigh's family, the Drapers, and Mike, they were becoming experts at rehoming the animals from the rescue operation. Joe and Hannah even managed to find homes in Seattle for a couple of the animals.

Until the weather started turning colder, Ryleigh hosted several campouts for her older niece and nephews. When Levi told his cousins about his campout with Jack and Sage, Aaron and Sophie insisted on joining him at Aunt Ryleigh's. They played games, ran with the dogs, and made s'mores over the firepit. Jack and Sage usually joined the kids in their tents instead of sleeping in the dog house. Ryleigh couldn't have been happier. They were bonding, making memories, and starting a new family tradition.

The upcoming wedding was always on her mind. When Ryleigh was ready to shop for a wedding dress, Amy's mom offered to take Allison and Levi for the day so Meghan, Ryleigh, Amy, and Emma could make a trip to Seattle. They met up with Spence's mom, and the ladies spent part of the day shopping for dresses. Since Ryleigh was pretty low maintenance, finding a suitable wedding dress didn't take long. Both mothers were able to find matching lavender dresses, while Amy and Emma found their matron of honor and bridesmaid dresses. Since the dress shopping went quickly, the ladies decided to treat themselves to a late lunch before heading home. Amy relished the girl time, knowing her kids were in good hands with Grandma Vicki.

As late summer quietly slipped into early autumn, the wedding was right around the corner before Ryleigh realized it. But she felt good about it. All the arrangements were in place, and Amy, Bailey, and Emma had helped her mail out the wedding invitations weeks ago.

Joe, Hannah, and Wyatt came over from Seattle to join the family in one more discussion to make sure all the bases had been covered. The family gathered at Aiden and Bailey's house for a large spaghetti feed and to get final headcounts.

"Ryleigh, have you received any more RSVPs in the last day or two?" Meghan asked. "Or do you think we have final headcounts?"

"No, I haven't," Ryleigh said. "So, I think we probably have everyone."

"Almost everyone," Joe said with a chuckle. "Mom called me this morning as we were leaving the house. She misplaced her invitation so wasn't sure how to RSVP. She wanted me to tell you and Spence that she will be coming down from Canada for the wedding. After missing the other wedding, she wants to make sure she's here for this one."

Spence squeezed Ryleigh's hand and said, "You're going to love Grandma Campbell."

"I can't wait to meet her," Ryleigh said. "She sounds like a lot of fun."

Sitting beside Matt, Emma laughed and said, "She's hilarious! And totally unpredictable."

"How is she unpredictable?" Ryleigh asked. "Most people her age are pretty set in their ways. And I don't mean that in a bad way."

Joe laughed and said, "My mother is definitely not set in her ways. I don't know a lot of women who actively participate in water fights well into their sixties. She's over seventy now, but I know she wouldn't hesitate to start a water fight if she had a chance!"

"What about the time she dragged the garden hose into the house to continue the water fight when the girls tried to hide from her?" Wyatt asked, laughing.

"Wait a minute!" Mike said, holding up his hand. "Are you saying, Wyatt, that your grandmother took a garden hose *into* the house and sprayed water around? That's a little hard to believe."

"But completely true, Mike," Joe nodded as he laughed. "My mother may try to convince people that she's all prim and proper, and she certainly can be when it's necessary. But, trust me, Lenora Sue Campbell is a force to be reckoned with!"

Mike sat back and smiled. "I've definitely got to meet that woman!"

"You'll all be able to meet her before long," Joe said. "She plans to come down about a week before the wedding to spend time with the family. I intend to spend some of that time trying to convince her to pack up and move down here. Nothing is holding her in Canada anymore, so she might as well be close to her family."

"Agreed," Spence said as he winked at Ryleigh. "I can think of several reasons for her to move down here."

* * *

With the wedding now only a couple of weeks away, and all the details handled, Ryleigh wanted to focus on setting up their house. Unwilling to infringe on Ryleigh's space before they were married, Spence still had all his belongings stored in the garage. It was time for that to change.

Ryleigh found Spence down at the shelter taking care of one of the new animals they had brought in the day before. He didn't notice her walk into the building, so Ryleigh stood back and watched him interact with the frightened animal.

"You're a natural, Spence," Ryleigh said, walking up to the cubicle where Spence sat on the floor stroking the young shepherd.

Spence smiled. "I didn't hear you come in."

Ryleigh joined him on the floor and reached over to pet the pup.

"You're great with the animals," Ryleigh said, smiling. "They feel safe with you. I remember you being that way with Coco when we first brought her in. I'm glad you like helping out here."

"Thanks for letting me help, Ryleigh."

"We're a team, remember? But we need to talk, Spence."

Spence looked at Ryleigh with concern. "What's wrong? Did I do something wrong with one of the animals?"

Ryleigh placed her hand on Spence's forearm and said, "No, Spence, you didn't do anything wrong." Grinning, she added, "It's what you haven't done that's the problem."

"Oh?"

"Spence, it's time to move your things into the house. I know you didn't want to infringe on my space before the wedding, but it's *our* house. It's not *my* house. I want you to get your belongings out of the garage and into the house. And put them wherever you want. Settle into *our* house. I don't know about you, but I sure don't want to be moving your things when we get back from our honeymoon. Just keep what you need at Emma's house until after the wedding, but please, move everything else into the house. Okay?"

Spence smiled at this woman he loved with all his heart. "Yes, dear. But is it okay to wait until Wyatt gets here tomorrow so he can help me?"

Ryleigh stood and started toward the door, grinning. "Okay, Mr. Campbell, you have until tomorrow. But before the weekend is over, I want all your things in the house. Got it?"

"Yes, ma'am!" Spence said as he hurried over to Ryleigh and pulled her into his arms. "Now, you have to give me a kiss. You know, to seal the deal."

As she reached up to kiss him, Ryleigh whispered, "You drive a hard bargain, Mr. Campbell."

* * *

As promised, when Wyatt and their parents arrived in town for the weekend, Spence recruited his brother to help move his things into the house. Since Spence and Ryleigh both worked from home, they agreed in advance to share the den as their workstation. So, Spence's priority was getting his desk, computer, and printer set up in the den. He would continue working with his laptop from his sister's house until after the honeymoon.

Before long, the boys had moved everything from the garage into the house. When Spence purposely left his suitcases and hanging clothes stacked against the wall in the living room, Ryleigh shook her head and pointed down the hall.

"Spence, please go hang your clothes in the bedroom closet," Ryleigh said, chuckling. "And unpack your suitcases. Everyone knows you're not moving in until after the wedding. Just unpack your clothes."

"Are you sure?" Spence asked.

"Yes, Spence, I'm sure," Ryleigh laughed as she pointed down the hall once again. "If it will make you feel better, I won't give you a key to the house until after the wedding."

There was a light knock on the front door before Travis and Meghan walked in, followed by Joe and Hannah.

"We came to see if you needed any help," Joe said, "but it looks like the garage is empty."

Ryleigh laughed as she pointed to the suitcases. "The only help I need is getting your son to put his clothes away!"

Hannah looked at her husband and laughed. "I suppose we should tell her that's never been one of Spencer's strong points."

Spence chuckled as he grabbed a suitcase. "I'm going. I'm going. Wyatt, grab some of those clothes and let's get them put away or we'll never hear the end of it!"

Wyatt laughed as he grabbed a stack of hanging clothes. "I don't know, Spence, I'd kind of like to see Ryleigh take you on. Smart money would be on the future Mrs. Campbell!"

The twins chuckled as they headed down the hall toward the bedroom, carrying clothes in both arms.

Within a few minutes, everyone had gathered in the living room to visit. Spence leaned over and kissed Ryleigh before joining her on the loveseat.

"So," Spence began, "did you guys find something else to talk about besides my clothes?"

Ryleigh squeezed Spence's hand and said, "They were wondering if we've decided where to go on our honeymoon."

Looking to Ryleigh for confirmation, Spence said, "I don't think we've made a final decision yet. We tossed around several ideas, but there are just so many cool places to go."

"You don't want to wait too long," Hannah said. "You'll need to make reservations."

Spence grinned before continuing. "Ireland is near the top of our list. But realistically, that's down the road a few years. Besides, we'd never be able to get any reservations in time. So, we narrowed it down and are trying to decide between a couple of different options."

"What are you thinking?" Travis asked.

"We're thinking about maybe going to Leavenworth to go skiing," Spence said.

"Or maybe going to Oregon to go to the beach," Ryleigh added. "We're just not sure. The beach could be cold in the middle of October, but it won't be crowded. But, mid-October might be a little early for good skiing."

"Why don't you go somewhere warmer?" Wyatt suggested. "Like California, or someplace."

Ryleigh and Spence looked at each other and smiled.

"Are you thinking what I'm thinking?" Spence asked.

"We were talking about next summer," Ryleigh said. "But it makes perfect sense to go in October."

Meghan laughed and said, "Don't keep us in suspense. Go where?"

"Disneyland!" Spence and Ryleigh yelled simultaneously.

"What better place to honeymoon than the 'happiest place on earth'?" Ryleigh said, smiling.

"Neither of us have been there since we were kids," Spence added. "It's perfect!"

"You're welcome…" Wyatt said, chuckling. "Since I gave you the idea, little brother, you have to give me your car."

Spence reached into his pocket, pulled out his car key, and tossed it to his brother. "Sounds like a fair trade. You get the car, and I get to honeymoon at Disneyland with my beautiful wife."

"Are you going to tell him you were already planning to give him the car?" Ryleigh asked, chuckling.

"Shhh!" Spence laughed. "He didn't need to know that!"

Chapter Twenty-Four

Lenora Sue Campbell arrived in Seattle a week before the wedding. Joe and Hannah picked her up at the airport and took her back to their townhouse for the day. She made it clear to her son that she had no desire to spend much time in Seattle. She always said, "City air stunts my growth." She wanted to check out the town of Hope and see her grandkids. The upcoming wedding was a happy by-product.

"Have you made reservations in Hope, son?" Lenora asked as soon as he sat her bags down in the entryway of the townhouse.

"Yes, mother," Joe laughed. "At Hotel Campbell."

"Hotel Campbell?"

Joe chuckled and explained, "The kids have plenty of room at their houses. Bailey and Aiden have a guest room, and so do Emma and Matt. And Meghan reminds us every time we go to Hope that they have lots of space at their house."

"Tell me again who Meghan is," Lenora said, laughing. "They have such a large family that it's hard for me to keep them all straight."

"Meghan and Travis are Ryleigh's parents," Joe explained.

"You're going to love them, Mom," Hannah told her mother-in-law. "They're wonderful people."

"Are you sure they have enough room?" Lenora asked. "There are four of us, with Wyatt."

Joe laughed as he took his mother's arm and led her to the living room. "Yes, mother, I'm sure. We have it all worked out. You can stay with Bailey and Aiden. Spence has been staying with Emma and Matt. Hannah, Wyatt, and I will be staying at Travis and Meghan's house. You worry too much. Just relax and enjoy the time with the family."

Lenora sat back in the recliner and put her feet up. "So, we're not going to Hope until tomorrow, huh?"

"Mom, we just got back from the airport," Joe said, smiling. "I promise to get you out of the city first thing in the morning. Okay?"

She closed her eyes and said, "That's good, Joe. You know the city air stunts my growth."

* * *

When Joe and Hannah came downstairs, they saw Lenora's suitcase sitting by the front door, with her purse prominently perched on top. Joe shook his head and chuckled just as they heard a noise coming from the kitchen.

"Either we have a large rat," Joe said, "or Mom is up to something in the kitchen."

Lenora sat a bowl of scrambled eggs and a plate of bacon on the table. Turning to her son and daughter-in-law, she said, "Pancakes are staying warm in the oven. I wondered when you two would be down."

Joe leaned down and kissed his mother on the cheek. "You realize it's only seven-thirty, don't you?"

"See, you nearly slept the morning away," Lenora chuckled as she took the plate of pancakes from the oven.

"Message received, mother," Joe laughed. "As soon as we wolf down this fantastic breakfast, we'll swing by the apartment and pick up Wyatt, then hit the road."

As Wyatt walked down the sidewalk toward the car, carrying his suitcase, Lenora rolled down the window and yelled out to her oldest grandson.

"Hurry up, boy!" Lenora laughed. "I'm slow, but I'm old!"

Wyatt put his suitcase in the back of the car, then leaned into the open car window and kissed his grandmother on the cheek.

"It's great to see you too, Grandma," Wyatt laughed.

"We can chitchat after we get on the road," Lenora said, grinning. "Get in the car!"

"Yes, ma'am!" Wyatt laughed, then quickly gave his grandmother another peck on the cheek.

Once they left the Seattle area and began heading up the pass, Joe brought up the subject of moving down from Canada.

Looking over at his mother in the passenger seat, he said, "Have you ever thought of leaving Canada, Mom?"

"What are you talking about, Joe? I just left Canada yesterday."

When Joe glanced in the rearview mirror, he saw his son grinning.

Joe shook his head and laughed. "That's not what I mean, Mom. Have you ever thought about moving down here? You would be a lot closer to your family."

"I'm not moving to Seattle, son. You know I don't like the city."

"Just think about it, okay, Mom?" Joe said quietly. "Dad's been gone for several years. You don't have anything tying you to Canada anymore. Someday you'll have great grandkids down here. That will be an entirely new generation of kids for you to spoil."

Lenora nodded. "You may have a point there. I do love spoiling the little ones. I'll give it some thought. But there's no way I'm moving to Seattle."

"Whatever you say, mother," Joe laughed. "I just want you to be happy. And I happen to know that spoiling babies makes you very happy."

* * *

As soon as the Campbell family pulled into Hope, Lenora began looking around from the passenger seat of her son's car. More than once she cautioned him to slow down, even though he was going below the posted speed limit, because she wanted to see the town.

At one point, she pointed to the side of the road and asked excitedly, "Is that an ice cream parlor?"

Joe nodded and said, "Yes, that's The Hope Creamery. The kids love going there."

"Pull over, Joe," his mother stated. "I want ice cream."

Wyatt chuckled from the back seat.

Joe laughed. "Don't you want to go see the kids and get settled in first?"

"We have all week to do that," Lenora laughed. "Let's get ice cream. Wyatt, text Spence and the girls and have them meet us at the ice cream parlor."

"Yes, Grandma," Wyatt laughed.

As Joe found a place to park, he laughed. "Ice cream in the middle of the morning. Sure, that makes perfect sense."

"Live a little, Joe," his mother chuckled. "All that city living is making you stuffy."

Even though everyone except Spence and Ryleigh was technically working, when Grandma Campbell summons you, you drop everything and go. Within twenty minutes, Spence and Ryleigh walked into The Creamery, followed by Bailey, Aiden, Emma, and Matt. Lenora immediately hugged her granddaughters and then looked at Aiden and Matt.

"You know the rules, boys," Lenora chuckled. "Everybody gets a hug from Grandma."

Aiden and Matt smiled, then hugged Grandma Campbell.

"It's good to see you again, Grandma," Aiden said.

"Did I ever thank you boys for bringing the girls by to visit when you were in Canada?"

Matt laughed. "Yes, you did. You thanked us several times, then sent us on our way with fresh brownies!"

Grandma Campbell stood with her hands on her hips, looking at Spence and Ryleigh. "Well, Spencer, I assume you're going to introduce me to your young lady?"

"Of course, Grandma," Spence laughed. "I had to wait until you finished with all your other hugs."

Looking at his future wife, Spence said, "Grandma, this is Ryleigh."

"Ryleigh," Grandma Campbell said, smiling. "That's a very pretty name. Irish, isn't it?"

"Yes, ma'am," Ryleigh said.

Grandma Campbell, who stood several inches shorter than Ryleigh, linked arms with her and started to the table where the others were seated. "You're going to sit by me, Ryleigh. I think we're going to be great friends. I need another granddaughter. And I don't want to hear any more of this 'yes, ma'am' business. You call me Grandma, just like the other kids."

"Yes, ma'am," Ryleigh instinctively replied. Then she laughed and corrected herself. "I mean, yes, Grandma."

Looking across the table at her youngest grandson, she laughed and said, "You better stay on your toes, Spence. Ryleigh's a quick learner!"

* * *

Over the next few days, as the wedding approached, there were several family gatherings, giving Lenora a chance to meet the rest of Ryleigh's family. She fell in love with everyone, but took a special interest in the kids. Aaron and Sophie captivated her when they invited her to play a game of cornhole with them. They laughed hysterically when she tossed the bag between her legs, nearly falling over, and it missed the board completely. One time she tossed the bag from behind her back. When the bag landed in the hole, both kids ran up and gave her a high-five.

Joe shook his head when his white-haired mother sat on the grass with her legs crossed, pulled little Levi into her lap, and began petting Jack and Sage.

"She'll eventually get around to getting to know the rest of you," Joe laughed. "But when she's around kids, all her attention is focused on them."

Hannah smiled and said, "Lenora is like the Pied Piper. All the kids follow her, and she loves it!"

Before long, Lenora joined the others on the back deck, with the kids trailing her, and walked over to Amy.

"Why don't you let me take the baby for a while, Amy?" Lenora asked. "I'll give you a little break."

Amy smiled as she handed her daughter over to Lenora, who had just given her 'a little break' an hour ago. "If she gets fussy, I can take her back."

"Oh, Allie and I will be just fine," Lenora said as she walked around in typical grandma fashion while rocking the baby.

"Won't we, Allie? You and Grandma Campbell are going to become best friends."

With her daughter safely in the hands of another grandma, Amy turned her attention to Ryleigh. "The wedding is in two days, Ryleigh. Is there anything else you need me to do? Are you guys all ready?"

"I think we're good to go," Ryleigh said. "You, Emma, and Bailey have been such a big help. There really wasn't anything for me to do. We're even already packed for Disneyland."

"Seriously?" Amy asked, chuckling.

"Sure," Ryleigh said. "It makes sense. The next two days are going to get busy really fast. I can imagine us on our way to the airport, then realizing our suitcases were sitting just inside the front door at home. I'm not taking that chance!"

Looking at his older sister, Spence asked, "Do you have everything you need from us, Bailey?"

"Well, if you could do something to settle my nerves, that would be awesome!" Bailey chuckled. Then she looked at Travis and asked, "Travis, are you sure I have everything ready to go? Since this is my first wedding, I don't want to forget something important."

Travis smiled and said, "You're going to do fine, Bailey. We've gone over what you want to say, and you'll have the formalities written down. All you need to do is relax. And in two days, your first wedding will be behind you."

Going over her mental checklist, Meghan said, "So, we have the rehearsal tomorrow afternoon. Then the rehearsal dinner is tomorrow night at the steak house. We can decorate the church right after the rehearsal. Isn't that what you two decided?"

"I think so," Ryleigh said, looking to Spence for confirmation.

"Yeah," Spence agreed. "It shouldn't take very long."

"Aunt Ryleigh," Sophie began, "are Sage and Jack going to the rehearsal too?"

"Of course, they are," Ryleigh said, smiling. "They have to rehearse their parts too, don't you think?"

"Yeah," Aaron agreed, "they'll need to practice. They aren't experienced like we are, Sophie."

"Wait a minute," Lenora said, holding up her hand. "Sage and Jack? Are you talking about the two dogs out there in the yard?"

"That's right, Grandma," Spence said, chuckling. "Ryleigh wants her two dogs to be part of the wedding."

"Dogs in a wedding," Lenora laughed as she sat back in the chair. "This is going to be a fun family!"

Chapter Twenty-Five

The rehearsal had gone well, and Sage and Jack had been on their best behavior. The two dogs took their roles seriously and seemed to know exactly what was expected. Sophie, Aaron, and Levi loved having the dogs at the rehearsal, and Levi tried hard not to distract them. As the rehearsal got underway, Bailey's nerves seemed to settle down. Everyone was impressed with the job she was doing officiating. It was a relaxed rehearsal, exactly what the young couple hoped for.

Once the rehearsal was over, the kids took Sage and Jack outside to play while the family began decorating the church. Neither Ryleigh nor Spence wanted anything elaborate for the wedding, so they knew it wouldn't take long. Meghan, Hannah, Amy, and Emma brought in all the flowers and set them up at the front of the church. Travis made sure the pastor's study was ready to use as a changing room for the bride and her attendants, and the elder's room was ready for Spence and Wyatt to use.

Before long, the family was gathering at Jackson's Steak House for the rehearsal dinner. As had become his custom, Mike insisted on hosting the rehearsal dinner. He had missed out on the family gatherings earlier in the week because he was out of town on business. As they were finishing up at the church, Mike texted

Travis to let him know he would be back in town in time for dinner.

Mike arrived at the steak house just as the others were seated in the banquet room. As he looked around the room, he found the empty chair Spence was saving for him next to Ryleigh. He took his seat and said hello to everyone. Looking toward Joe and Hannah, his eyes landed on the only person who was a stranger to him.

"There seems to be a young lady at the end of the table I haven't met," Mike said, smiling.

Joe put his hand on his mother's forearm and said, "Mike, this is my mother, Lenora Campbell. Mom, this is Mike Slater. You've heard us talk about him."

Mike tipped his head at Lenora, smiled, and said, "So, I finally get to meet the infamous Lenora Sue Campbell. It's my pleasure, Ms. Campbell."

Lenora chuckled and said, "I'm not sure about being infamous. But it's a pleasure to meet you, Mike. I understand you're hosting this dinner, so just know I plan to eat my weight in appetizers!"

Joe groaned as he slapped his forehead. "Mother, can't you behave for five minutes?"

"Where's the fun in that?" Lenora asked, laughing.

Mike laughed. "I look forward to visiting with you a little more after the wedding tomorrow."

Turning to the rest of the family, Mike added, "Sorry I wasn't available to help out with things this week. Is everything ready for tomorrow's big event?"

"The church is decorated, and the clothes are already at the church," Meghan said. "The only thing left is marrying off my last child."

Ryleigh laughed. "I'll try to make it as painless as possible, Mom."

* * *

The wedding day had arrived, and Hope Community Church was a hub of activity. The mothers of the young couple, as well as the bride's attendants, were dressed and ready to go. They were gathered in the pastor's study while Amy helped Ryleigh into her wedding dress. Hannah and Vicki took turns entertaining the baby so Amy could focus on Ryleigh.

As Amy adjusted the veil on Ryleigh's head, Meghan covered her mouth with her hands, then whispered, "You're beautiful, Ryleigh. Just like Kaci. It's been a long time since your sister's wedding. Now, my baby girl is getting married. I'm so happy for you, honey."

Ryleigh took her mother's hand and said, "Now, mother, you can't be making me cry right before my wedding. I'm sure Amy doesn't want to redo my makeup."

Meghan chuckled and said, "You said you would try to make this as painless as possible, so I'll try to save the tears until your vows. But I make no promises!"

Ryleigh stood back and looked at her reflection in the floor-length mirror. "Well, ladies, do you think I'm ready to go?"

Amy smiled and said, "I think our work here is done."

Just then, there was a light tap on the door and Kaci poked her head into the room.

"If you're ready, sis," Kaci said, "I believe it's time. And you are absolutely beautiful!"

"Thanks, Kaci. How are Sage and Jack doing?" Ryleigh asked.

"Ryleigh, you need to relax and focus on yourself," Kaci said, smiling. "Uncle Todd has taken charge of the dogs, and they're doing great. The kids are great. Everyone is ready to go. And Dad is waiting in the hall for you."

"Well, okay, then," Ryleigh said, chuckling. "If everyone's great, then it must be time. What do you say, ladies, shall we do this?"

"Absolutely!" Amy said enthusiastically. Then leaning toward her best friend, she said quietly, "I'm so happy for you, Ryleigh. You deserve a great guy like Spence. As your dad always says, 'God is good.' And that's so true."

"It certainly is," Ryleigh said. "Thanks, Amy. For everything."

The ladies began lining up in the foyer as Travis walked over to his youngest daughter and took her by the hand.

"You know, Ryleigh," Travis began, "you've had an interesting and challenging time since you finished school. But through it all, you managed to stay true to yourself. You know who you are and what's important to you. I'm really proud of you, kiddo. I can't believe everything you've accomplished in the past year. You never cease to amaze me. I love you."

"I love you too, Dad," Ryleigh said. "I already told Mom not to make me cry before my wedding, so you can't either."

"In that case, my dear child, put a smile on that beautiful face, and let's go get you married off!"

As Travis and Ryleigh stepped away from the sanctuary doors, the doors opened, and the attendants started up the aisle. They were followed by Aaron holding the ring pillow and Sophie spreading flower petals. Once the kids were inside the sanctuary, the doors closed. Todd stood beside Sage and Jack, ready to start the dogs down the aisle ahead of Ryleigh and Travis.

Todd knelt beside the dogs and whispered, "Remember, just how we practiced yesterday. It's your time to shine for Ryleigh and Spence, okay? Make them proud. You're good dogs."

Before standing, he petted Sage and Jack on their heads, unclipped their leashes, and sent up a quick prayer.

When the wedding march began, Travis looked at Ryleigh and smiled. "Well, kiddo, are you ready?"

"Let's do this, Dad," Ryleigh said, smiling.

The doors to the sanctuary opened once again. Sage stood next to Jack, wearing a lavender scarf to match Ryleigh's colors. Jack was wearing a lavender vest and black bowtie. At Todd's urging, the dogs looked at each other, held their heads high, and looked straight ahead before entering the sanctuary.

The family were the only ones who knew the dogs would be taking part in the ceremony. All the guests were smiling at the surprise, many nodding as they realized it couldn't have been any other way.

Travis tucked Ryleigh's hand into the crook of his arm and followed Sage and Jack toward the pulpit. When the dogs reached the front of the sanctuary, they stepped to the side and sat watching Ryleigh and Travis come down the aisle. Travis kissed his daughter on the cheek, put her hand in Spence's hand, then took his seat next to Meghan.

Standing in front of the pulpit, Bailey looked at the dogs and smiled. "If you'd told me a year ago that two dogs would walk down the aisle in my first wedding, I never would have believed you. But, after getting to know Ryleigh, it makes perfect sense."

Looking at Spence, she continued. "A few years ago, I never would have imagined that someday I would officiate my little brother's wedding. But God works in mysterious ways, and here we are."

Bailey continued by giving the young couple some advice Travis had shared at her wedding not long ago, along with some passages from the Bible regarding marriage.

"Spence and Ryleigh have written their vows," Bailey said, glancing at her brother. "They haven't shared them with me, so I'll be hearing them for the first time along with you.

"Spence, you can go first," Bailey said.

Spence nervously took a piece of paper out of his breast pocket. He looked at it, shook his head, and tucked it back in the pocket.

Turning to Ryleigh, Spence swallowed before speaking. "I had everything written down, but it seems kind of corny. I think I just want to tell you how I feel."

Looking at Bailey, he asked, "Is that okay?"

Bailey nodded and said, "Speak from your heart, Spence. You'll do fine."

"Ryleigh, I never thought I would be lucky enough to be standing here, waiting to become your husband. You are the most amazing person I know. You have such a big heart. I've never known anyone who would fall down a mountain for a dog, but I honestly believe there is nothing you wouldn't do to help an animal in need. Your love has no boundaries. It doesn't stop with family, and it doesn't stop with animals. You love all living beings. That's part of what makes you special. I love you, Ryleigh, and I can't wait to see what adventures we'll have together."

Bailey smiled at her brother and said, "Well done, Spence."

Turning to Ryleigh, she said, "Okay, Ryleigh, your turn."

Ryleigh looked at Spence with love in her eyes. "Spence, I knew you were special the first time we met. But I think I fell in love with you when I saw how completely you accepted who I was when I struggled with living away from my family. You hoped I would fall in love with Seattle, but you didn't try to talk me into staying there. I didn't fall in love with Seattle. I fell in love with you, and that's so much better. When I saw the compassion you have for animals, and how safe they feel with you, I knew you were the man God had chosen for me. I love you so much, Spence. And I promise our lives will be filled with adventures."

Then she chuckled, adding, "They'll probably all involve animals, but I'm pretty sure you're okay with that."

"Wow," Bailey said, nodding. "You two definitely belong together."

Bailey nodded to Amy and Wyatt, who took the rings from Aaron.

Turning to her brother, Bailey said, "Spencer James Campbell, do you take this woman to be your lawfully wedded wife?"

Looking into Ryleigh's eyes, Spence replied, "I do."

Bailey turned to Ryleigh and said, "Ryleigh Elizabeth Harmon, do you take this man to be your lawfully wedded husband?"

Smiling at Spence, Ryleigh said, "Yes, I do."

Bailey nodded to Wyatt, and he handed Spence the ring for Ryleigh.

"Spence," Bailey said, "place the ring on Ryleigh's finger and repeat after me. 'With this ring, I thee wed.'"

Spence slid the ring onto Ryleigh's finger and repeated, "With this ring, I thee wed."

Amy handed Spence's ring to Ryleigh.

"Ryleigh," Bailey said, "place the ring on Spence's finger and repeat after me. 'With this ring, I thee wed.'"

After starting to put the ring on the wrong finger, Ryleigh chuckled as she slid the ring onto Spence's finger and said, "With this ring, I thee wed."

Bailey quickly glanced at Travis to be sure she hadn't forgotten anything, then turned back to the couple. "I now pronounce you husband and wife. Spence, you may kiss your bride."

Spence took Ryleigh into his arms and kissed her tenderly, then the young couple turned to face the guests.

"Ladies and gentlemen," Bailey began, "I present Mr. and Mrs. Spencer Campbell!"

Spence and Ryleigh clasped hands and raised them in the air. Sage and Jack barked loudly and wagged their tails happily before turning and leading the newlyweds down the aisle and out of the sanctuary.

Chapter Twenty-Six

Shortly after the wedding, everyone gathered in the fellowship hall at the church to take pictures. Lots of family pictures were taken, as well as the traditional pictures of the bride and groom cutting the wedding cake. Still dressed in their wedding attire, Ryleigh made sure the photographer took several photos of her and Spence with Sage and Jack. She also wanted a picture of the two dogs with Aaron, Sophie, and Levi. Mike chuckled when he saw Lenora photobomb the picture of the dogs with the kids. Joe laughed and shook his head, not at all surprised by his mother's antics.

Spence walked over and took his grandma by the hand.

"Come on, Grandma," Spence said, laughing. "I want an official picture of you with me and Ryleigh, all the kids, and Sage and Jack."

Then he leaned over and whispered to her, "But I plan to enlarge and frame the picture you photobombed."

"I'm going to need a copy of that, Spence," Lenora said with a grin.

Sage and Jack quickly became the hit of the photo session and pranced around proudly in their scarf and vest.

When the bride and groom were ready to change clothes after the photo session, Ryleigh leaned down to remove Sage's scarf. Sage pulled back and stood beside Jack, who also refused to have his vest and tie removed.

Spence laughed and said, "I guess there's no reason they can't wear their wedding duds until the end of the day. After all, it's been a special occasion for them."

"You're right," Ryleigh smiled. "And they seem to be enjoying all the extra attention. But, I'm changing into jeans and a top before I join the reception."

"I'm right behind you, Mrs. Campbell," Spence said. "You know, I like the sound of that."

Ryleigh stopped to kiss her new husband and said, "So do I, Mr. Campbell." Then she lifted the skirt of her wedding dress and ran down the hall to change clothes.

* * *

Ryleigh and Spence returned to the reception to find everyone seated at tables around the room visiting, but no one had touched the food.

Spence picked up a glass and tapped it with a fork from the buffet table to get everyone's attention.

"We've already told everyone this is a very informal reception," Spence said, grinning. "We expected you to work your way through the food line. And Wyatt, bro, I'm disappointed in you. I thought I could count on you to be at the head of the line."

Wyatt laughed. "I started to, then Grandma smacked me on the back of the head. She said, 'No one eats before the bride and groom.' So, little brother, if you want to take it up with Grandma, be my guest!"

"I think I'll pass," Spence laughed. Taking his bride by the hand, he said, "Okay, Ryleigh and I are going to grab plates and start eating. Everyone else can get in line – behind Grandma!"

The kids hurried over to Lenora, knowing she would be at the head of the line.

Sophie took her hand and said, "Come on, Grandma. You have to get in line behind Aunt Ryleigh and Uncle Spence. We'll get in line right behind you."

Lenora allowed the kids to lead her to the food table. She leaned over and whispered, "Did you notice there are chocolate chip cookies *and* cake? I'm going to get both. What about you kids?"

Aaron and Sophie looked at each other and grinned.

Before they could reply, Levi reached up and tugged on Lenora's free hand. "Grandma, I want both."

"You stick with me, Levi," Lenora said, grinning. "I'll make sure you get both."

Joe and Hannah got in line behind the kids. Joe laughed and asked, "Mother, are you corrupting these kids?"

Three-year-old Levi looked up at Joe and asked, "What's 'rupting?"

Travis and Meghan laughed as they fell in line behind Joe and Hannah.

Meghan said, "It means spoiling, Levi. And, yes, Grandma Campbell is spoiling you kids. But it's okay because today is a special occasion. And spoiling kids is a grandma's job."

Aaron looked at Meghan and asked, "Does that mean we get to have cake *and* a cookie, Grandma?"

"If you want both, and will eat it," Meghan grinned. "But just for today. You aren't going to make a habit of eating two desserts."

Joe chuckled as he shook his head. When it came to his mother and kids, anyone's kids, he knew he was fighting an uphill battle.

Before long, everyone had a plate of food, found a table, and continued visiting. Mike walked up to a table where Lenora and her grandkids were sitting.

"Do you kids mind if I join you?" Mike asked.

"You're always welcome, Mike," Matt said. "Grab a chair."

As he sat down, he looked across the table at Lenora and said, "I was hoping we'd get a chance to visit after the wedding."

"Since Grandma doesn't get down from Canada very often, we've been reminiscing and talking about all the crazy things Grandma does," Emma said, laughing.

"I object!" Lenora said. "I do not do crazy things. I have a little fun occasionally, but I do not do crazy things. You know, Emma, you kids are getting older. Your memories probably aren't very reliable."

Spence shook his head and said, "I don't know, Grandma, you've been known to do a few, uh, interesting things."

With a fork in her hand, in between bites of food, Lenora waved her hand dismissively. "Mike, don't you dare believe a word these kids say about me. They all have wild imaginations."

"I don't know, Lenora Sue," Mike said, grinning. "I've already witnessed a few of your, shall we say, personality quirks today. If the kids have wild imaginations, what about Joe? Can I believe what he says about you?"

"Uh-oh, Grandma," Wyatt chuckled. "He may have found a loophole."

"Oh, phooey," Lenora retorted. "He has found no such thing."

"So," Mike began again, chuckling, "what about Joe? Is he a reliable source of information?"

"I doubt it," Lenora said, grinning. "He can't be trusted either."

"Well, let's see," Mike said. "So, it's not true that you start water fights?"

"Okay, that might possibly be true," Lenora laughed. "I've been known to start a little water fight when it's hot outside."

"Hmm. Outside brings up an interesting question," Mike said, thoroughly enjoying himself. "So, you've never dragged a garden hose *into* the house to finish a water fight?"

"Well…" Lenora hedged. "Only the one time."

"And I don't suppose you've ever raced the kids down the street on a skateboard?" Mike continued his playful interrogation.

"Okay," Lenora nodded. "Maybe you can believe some of what they say. But certainly not everything!"

"And I seem to remember hearing about some Halloween pranks," Mike said. "I suppose those stories are fabricated as well?"

Lenora looked around the table at her grandkids and said, "You kids have nothing better to do than sit around telling stories? You all need to find hobbies!"

By now, several others had crowded around to listen to the stories.

"You know, Grandma," Spence began mischievously, as he nudged Ryleigh, "since we just had a wedding, would you care to tell Mike why you weren't able to make it down for Bailey and Emma's wedding?"

"I was laid up with a broken leg, Mike," Lenora said, waving her hand. "End of story."

Showing concern, Mike said, "I'm so sorry, Lenora Sue. That had to be difficult for you."

All her grandkids chuckled, and Joe laughed out loud.

"And how did you get that broken leg, Mom?" Joe asked, laughing.

"I played on a senior league softball team. Things happen."

"And?" Joe continued, knowing his mother was enjoying this as much as he was.

"And, I broke my leg sliding into third base," Lenora said with a shrug.

"My word, Lenora Sue!" Mike said, shaking his head. "Why did you decide to slide?"

"I couldn't let them tag me!"

"But, Grandma," Emma said, chuckling, "you broke your leg!"

"But, *Emma*, I was safe!"

Mike, along with everyone else, roared in laughter.

By now, with music playing in the background, several couples had taken to the dance floor.

Still laughing, Mike stood and walked around the table to Lenora. "If your leg has sufficiently healed, Lenora Sue, would you care to dance?"

Pushing back her chair, Lenora answered, "I'd love to, Mike. I've never broken a leg dancing!"

Laughing, Mike took Lenora by the hand and headed to the dance floor.

Walking away from the table, she said, "Hey, I wonder if I can still do the jitterbug?"

Mike looked back at Joe with a deer-in-the-headlights look.

Joe shrugged and said, "Good luck, Mike!"

Spence took Ryleigh by the hand and led her to the dance floor.

"I'm glad your grandma was able to come down for the wedding," Ryleigh said as they began dancing.

Spence looked across the room to see his grandma and Mike laughing as they danced. "Maybe now she'll move down here."

"Well," Ryleigh said, smiling, "as Bailey said, 'God works in mysterious ways.'"

Epilogue

Four Months Later

Bundled up to ward off the February chill, Joe and Hannah Campbell stood on the sidewalk in front of Phase II of the Hope Estates Development waiting to meet with Mike Slater. A few minutes later, Mike pulled up along the curb in an R & M Development pickup. Mike climbed out of the truck, walked over, shook hands with Joe, and hugged Hannah.

"How was the drive over the pass, Joe?" Mike asked.

"It wasn't too bad," Joe replied. "Lots of snow along the road, but the roads were all bare and wet. Can't ask for much more than that in the middle of February."

"Can I assume you both recovered from the Christmas holidays?" Mike asked with a chuckle.

Smiling, Hannah said, "I don't know when I've had so much fun at Christmas! The kids married into such a wonderful family. I never gave much thought to leaving Seattle before, but now I can't wait to be closer to all the kids."

"That family does have a way of growing on you," Mike laughed. "What about your mother, Joe? Is she on board with moving down here?"

Laughing, Joe said, "I never would have been able to convince her to move to Seattle. Moving to Hope was an easy sell. She didn't even care if Hannah and I moved over here. She said she would have been perfectly happy staying with the kids."

Mike chuckled, then said, "I have a couple of houses in mind to show you. One is two doors down from here, and the other is up around the corner. Both houses were just recently finished."

"Lead the way, Mike," Joe said. "Did Aiden and Matt build these two houses as well?"

"Yes, they did," Mike confirmed. "Those boys are making a name for themselves around the area. And they've put together good crews."

Joe took his wife by the hand and followed Mike to the first house, a single-level home with a nice open floor plan.

"I love that most of the houses have a nice deck on the back side. Our townhouse only has a small balcony, which isn't really functional. After seeing the decks on the kids' houses, it makes family get-togethers so much nicer."

Joe and Hannah made mental notes of some of their favorite features in the first house, then followed Mike down the block to the second home.

As they walked up the sidewalk to the two-story house, Mike said, "I think you'll like this house too. It has some design features that could make it perfect for you guys."

Mike opened the front door and led them into the main living area.

"Joe," Hannah said, taking her husband's hand, "look at that beautiful fireplace. And I love the open concept. You can see right out onto the back deck."

"Before we look around," Mike began, "let me tell you about some things that could make this house a perfect fit for you. There is a master suite down here on the main floor. That could easily work for your mother, Joe. There's a second master suite upstairs, along with two additional bedrooms. That would provide plenty of room for you two, and Wyatt until he flies the coop. This floor plan is perfect for multi-generational families."

After spending nearly an hour wandering through the house and thinking out loud about how to utilize the space, the three met back down in the main living area.

"So," Mike began, "what did you think of the two houses?"

"They're both great houses, Mike," Joe said. "You can tell the boys take pride in their work."

Turning to his wife, Joe asked, "What do you think, honey?"

Hannah looked at her husband and said, "I liked the first house, but I love this house, Joe. I think it's perfect for us. I really do."

Joe pulled Hannah into his arms and hugged her tightly. "I agree, honey. It's perfect. Mom will love having her own space. And Wyatt is so easygoing. As long as he has a place to set up his computer to work, he's not very fussy."

"So?" Hannah asked, her eyes silently pleading for a positive response.

Joe reached out to shake hands with Mike.

"We'll take it, Mike!"

Mike smiled and said, "Welcome to Hope!"

* * *

Six weeks later Joe and Hannah pulled a large U-Haul truck into Hope and made their way across town to their new home. Driving his parents' car, with his grandma in the passenger seat, Wyatt parked behind the truck. Lenora had flown down to Seattle after packing up her house in Canada. The double move was a logistical nightmare, but with the help of lots of family, they thought they had a plan.

It was late afternoon by the time they arrived in Hope. Since they had already loaded the truck that morning, Joe said they would wait until the next day to unload their belongings. Meghan and Kaci had planned a big spaghetti dinner for everyone, knowing they would be exhausted.

After enjoying a filling dinner, everyone gathered in the living room to discuss the plans for the next day.

"Joe," Travis began, "the whole family is available to help. You just let us know what you need."

Letting out an exhausted sigh, Joe said, "Thanks, Travis. What I really need is some sleep! We certainly appreciate everyone's help. Let's see if we can come up with a game plan for tomorrow. Wyatt and I were discussing some of it last night, so we at least know what needs to be done."

"I can drive your car up to Grandma's house in the morning, Dad," Wyatt said. "We'll need someone to drive Grandma's car back and someone to drive the moving truck. Plus, we're going to need to load the truck first. So, I'll need some help with that."

"Ryleigh and I can go with you, Wyatt," Spence said.

"It will go faster if you have another set of hands," Todd added. "As long as there's room for four people in the car, I can ride up with you and help load the truck. I can drive it back if you want me to, unless one of you boys would rather drive it."

"Thanks, Todd," Spence said. "That will be a big help. Ryleigh, if you don't mind driving Grandma's car back, then one of us can drive Dad and Mom's car, and maybe the other two could trade off driving the truck."

"Sure, I can do that," Ryleigh agreed.

"Aiden and Matt," Travis said, "can you boys help us unload Joe's truck tomorrow?"

"Sure," Matt said. "Just tell us what time to be there."

"Do you want us to round up some of the guys from work to help?" Aiden asked.

"I think we'll probably be fine," Travis said. "But if you have any guys hanging around looking for something to do, we won't turn down extra help."

"Is there anything I can help with, Joe?" Mike asked.

"Maybe you can keep my mother entertained while we unload the truck," Joe laughed. "She tends to be a Monday Morning Quarterback."

Mike laughed. "It will be my pleasure. Lenora Sue, I'll pick you up in the morning and we'll go have breakfast. That should keep us both out of trouble."

"I wouldn't count on it, Mike!" Lenora laughed.

* * *

After a couple of hectic weeks, with everyone pitching in to help, the entire Campbell clan was finally settled in Hope. Hannah began checking out the town, and Joe let out an internal sigh of relief knowing his elderly mother would be right under his roof. Wyatt quickly found the local electronics store and stocked up on some games. He also discovered a hamburger place and soon claimed it as his favorite burger joint. Lenora wasted no time figuring out where the kids in the family lived. She had big plans to take them all out for ice cream whenever she could sneak them away.

Since the weather had been unseasonably warm, Spence and Ryleigh planned an early-season barbecue at their house. Spence and Wyatt set up the badminton net and Travis brought the cornhole game over. Aaron talked Uncle Matt into bringing his baseball glove so they could play catch. Jack and Sage spent the afternoon chasing each other around the yard and playing with the kids.

Ryleigh noticed her Aunt Nicole watching the dogs intently.

"Aunt Nicole," Ryleigh said, smiling, "you and Uncle Todd should get a dog. My shelter is nearly full again, you know."

"Ryleigh," Nicole began, "I love you, girl, but we don't need a dog."

"Need is such a *strong* word," Ryleigh chuckled. "You know you're going to be retiring soon. A dog could help fill all that free time you would have."

"The point of retiring is to have free time that's not claimed by someone or something," Nicole said with a grin. "Besides, what would I do with a dog?"

Ryleigh gave her aunt one of her best pleading looks, then said, "You would be giving a sweet puppy a loving home."

"Have you ever thought of going into politics, Ryleigh?" Nicole asked, laughing, as she shook her head, then headed out to the back yard.

"Hey, you can't blame a girl for trying!" Ryleigh shouted after her.

In the meantime, Grandma Campbell entertained everyone on the badminton court when she insisted on using her racket like a baseball bat. Mike chuckled whenever Aaron or Sophie walked over and tried to show her how to hold a badminton racket properly.

"No, no, Aaron," Grandma said. "Holding it that way may work for you kids, but if you hold it my way, you can hit a home run!"

Aaron shook his head and laughed. "Grandma, home runs are in baseball, not badminton."

"Home runs *could* be in badminton if you kids would hold the racket my way," Grandma laughed as she handed him her racket and went to join the adults on the deck.

Lenora sat in a deck chair next to Mike and reached over to pet Coco, who was curled up on Mike's lap.

"I keep meaning to ask you, Mike," Lenora began, "where did you get that sweet little dog?"

"Coco was one of the first dogs Ryleigh rescued and brought into her operation," Mike said as he petted his constant companion. "She had been scheduled to be put down when Ryleigh came to the rescue."

Lenora looked at Ryleigh, sitting beside Spence on the loveseat. "How many animals do you have at Ryleigh's Rescue?"

"We currently have five dogs and a mama cat with her kitten," Ryleigh said.

"And you can find homes for all the animals you rescue?" Lenora asked.

"We do," Ryleigh nodded. "The whole family, along with Mike and the local vets, have gotten really good at finding homes for the animals."

"Do you help Ryleigh with the rescue operation, Spence?" Lenora asked.

"Yes, I do," Spence said. "It's great seeing these animals go from hopeless situations to loving homes."

Lenora was quiet for a few moments before turning to her son. "Joe, can I have a dog?"

Joe chuckled. "Whatever you want, Mom. I just want you to be happy."

Smiling widely, Lenora asked, "Ryleigh, do you think you and Spence can find a dog for me?"

Spence looked at Ryleigh, smiled, and said, "Penelope!"

The young couple jumped up and each took one of Lenora's hands. "Come on, Grandma," Ryleigh said excitedly. "We've got the perfect dog for you!"

Within a few minutes, the kids started running toward Ryleigh's Rescue, with Sage and Jack racing alongside. Ryleigh and Spence hurried Grandma across the back yard, followed by the rest of the family.

Spence pointed to a chair along the wall and said, "Have a seat, Grandma. We'll be right back."

Before long, Ryleigh came out of one of the cubicles carrying a small white poodle.

Placing the dog in Lenora's arms, Ryleigh said, "Grandma, meet Penelope."

Holding the little dog up to her face, Lenora peered through her glasses, looked into the dog's eyes, and said, "Well, aren't you just the cutest little thing? I hope you like kids and babies, Miss Penelope. And you're going to have to get acquainted with Miss Coco. I suspect we'll be seeing a lot of her."

About that time, Nicole walked out of one of the cubicles at the far end of the building. She was cradling a German Shepherd puppy and grinning widely.

Todd looked at his wife, with his hands on his hips. Wearing a small smile, he said, "Nicole, honey, we talked about this. We don't need a dog. Remember?"

Glancing at her niece, Nicole smiled and said, "Need is such a *strong* word."

Laughing, Ryleigh raised her arm in victory, and yelled, "Yes!"

"Ryleigh…" Todd began. "We need to talk, kiddo."

Travis walked up behind his brother-in-law, slapped him on the back, and laughed, "Need is such a *strong* word, Todd."

"Don't worry, Uncle Todd," Ryleigh said, trying unsuccessfully to hide a grin. "We'll throw in the first bag of puppy chow."

Turning to Ryleigh, Grandma chuckled and said, "So, you just go around rescuing animals and making everyone's lives better?"

Ryleigh smiled as she put her arm around Spence's waist and said, "Yes, ma'am, Grandma. It's what we do."

~ The End ~